The Place Where Nobody Stopped

This particular morning, just two steps outside the door, Yosip the Baker stopped walking, and this was very strange. Never before had he stopped on the way to the road.

I don't know why he stopped. Even Yosip didn't know. But he felt as if something were going to happen today, something that had never happened before in the place where nobody stopped.

Perhaps it was the forest, or the woodchoppers' houses, or the muddy road. He looked at the sleeping forest, at his neighbors' shabby dwellings among the trees, at the empty road. No. They were just as they always were. In his mind, Yosip examined his body. Did his back hurt? No. His head, his arms, his legs, his feet? No, no, no, and no.

Shaking his head in befuddlement, he continued toward the road, put the bags in their usual place for the stagecoach to pick up, and returned to his kitchen.

But all day long, as he sifted, measured, mixed, and kneaded, Yosip the Baker felt a strange anticipation fluttering in his round stomach. Why did he feel that this day was different from all other days?

·The Place Where Nobody Stopped·

JERRY SEGAL

illustrations by
DAV PILKEY

A BEECH TREE PAPERBACK BOOK
New York

Printed in the United States of America.
First edition published in 1991 by Orchard Books.
First Beech Tree Edition, 1994.
Published by arrangement with Orchard Books.
Text design by Mina Greenstein
10 9 8 7 6 5 4 3 2 1

The Library of Congress Cataloging-in-Publication Data
Segal, Jerry
The place where nobody stopped / Jerry Segal.
p. cm. "A Richard Jackson book"
Summary: A Jewish man plants himself in a lonely Russian baker's house and establishes a family while waiting for permission to go to America.
ISBN 0-688-12567-0 (pbk.)
[1. Soviet Union—Fiction. 2. Jews—Soviet Union—Fiction.]
I. Pilkey, Dav. 1966- ill. II. Title
PZ7.S45255P1 1994 [Fic]—dc20 94-86
CIP
AC

because of Ann . . .

1

IN Russia there is a very old and very famous dirt road. But I must tell you, when it began its life over a thousand years ago, it wasn't famous. It wasn't even a road. It was a narrow, sandy footpath.

As century after century passed, however, the boots and sandals and wooden shoes of countless travelers, the crushing wheels of wagons and carts and carriages, and the pounding, grinding hooves of horses and oxen made this road of ours so wide and so deep that a small child standing on tiptoe could barely see over its sides.

Russians who wanted to travel from east to west—or from west to east, depending on which way they were going—always used this ancient and distinguished road of ours. Genghis Khan and his ruthless Golden Horde, on their way to destroy eastern Europe, stormed down this road. When Ivan the Terrible invaded and terrorized Poland, he led his murderous cavalry along this road. The beaten and retreating soldiers of Napoleon the Great froze to death on this road. And since the very beginning of Russia, whenever the Czar traveled from Moscow to Riga—or from Riga to Moscow—on what do you think his Imperial Majesty traveled? That's right: on our road.

But I'm sorry to say that even though our road passed through lovely meadows and forests and fertile groves of fruit and fields of grain, it was a very dangerous road. When the deadly Russian winter roared in from the North Pole, our road froze into a treacherous river of ice, whipped by arctic winds and blocked by huge snowdrifts. In the spring, floods changed our road into an impassable swamp. In the summer, scorching, choking clouds of dust billowed up from its bed. And in the fall, sometimes you couldn't even find it—a thick quilt of dying leaves hid long stretches of our road from sight.

TWO large cities, Vitebsk and Smolensk, sat on this road, less than a day's journey apart. When travelers journeyed from Vitebsk to Smolensk—or from Smolensk to Vitebsk, depending on which way they were going—they always shouted, "Onward to Vitebsk before nightfall, with no stopping in between," or, "Onward to Smolensk before nightfall, with no stopping in between."

Turning neither to the right nor the left, they followed our road straight from one city to the other, hurrying as fast as they could, traveling only in the daytime. No one ever stopped between Vitebsk and Smolensk.

And yet, halfway between these two cities, neither closer to Vitebsk than to Smolensk, nor closer to Smolensk than to Vitebsk, there *was* a place.

Why do I call it a "place" instead of the village of such-and-such or the town of so-and-so? Because this pitiful group of humble dwellings, half-hidden among the trees at the edge of the forest, had no name. People called it "the place where nobody stops."

When rich travelers saw this dismal spot from their carriage windows, they wrinkled their noses in disdain and closed their shades. Riders on horseback, nearing the place where nobody stopped, whipped their mounts to make them go faster.

Even the lowliest voyagers traveling on foot crossed themselves, spat on the ground, and quickened their steps as they passed these wretched houses, thinking to themselves, "Surely this lonely place is haunted. I've been through here many times and have never seen a single human being. Only ghosts and demons must live in those desolate shacks scattered among the trees."

But, of course, the travelers were wrong. Human beings *did* live in the place where nobody stopped.

EXCEPT for Yosip the Baker, the residents of the place where nobody stopped were a handful of poor woodchoppers and their families, peasants who had lived for generations in the same timeworn, straw-thatched, tumbledown, clay-patched log cabins.

Only Yosip the Baker owned a stone house with plaster walls, and even though I wouldn't call it a castle, that's what it looked like compared to the peasants' huts. Many years earlier, he had come to the place where nobody stopped, looked around until he found a suitable location near the road, gone back to Vitebsk and rented the piece of land from the Czar's agent, returned to the place where nobody stopped with wagons full of building materials and bakers' tools, and himself constructed a modest one-room cottage big enough to hold his large stone oven, his barrels of flour and kegs of sugar, his cupboard for wooden spoons and spatulas and bowls and measuring cups, his cabinets that held yeast and molasses and raisins, his underground larder for eggs and milk and butter, his oversize round table on which he mixed, kneaded, and shaped the dough, and enough floor space to lay the loaves out to cool after they were baked.

In no time the woodchoppers and their families became fond of Yosip the Baker. It's true that he seldom spoke. Most of the time he kept to himself, staying inside his house as if it were a prison and he a criminal serving a sentence. But when a neighbor needed help, good-hearted and soft-spoken Yosip the Baker was the first to offer aid. He brought soup and medicine to the ill. If ever a woodchopper's only goat died, Yosip offered him a kid from his own tiny herd. He paid the children shiny copper kopeks for gathering kindling or fetching eggs from his henhouse or milking his cows. And every morning, before he filled several large canvas bags with bread and cakes for the Smolensk-to-Vitebsk stagecoach to pick up for his customers in the city, this strange and quiet man set aside a dozen or so loaves of bread for his half-starved neighbors. In exchange, since the proud peasants insisted on working for their food, the children and women went into the forest and gathered sweet berries

---

At night Yosip the Baker sat by himself in his silent, empty house.

from which Yosip made syrup for his babkas, and nuts whose meats he crushed into a paste to flavor his cake dough. So although he lived like a hermit and spoke only when necessary, Yosip the Baker was accepted as a friend and blessed by his poor neighbors, the serfs. Thanks to him, every day a loaf of fresh bread graced every table in the place where nobody stopped.

What the woodchoppers and their families did not know was that each night, after the men came home to their families from the forest, and the sounds of people talking and babies crying and children laughing emanated from their scattered hovels and drifted faintly through the darkened trees toward Yosip the Baker's house, he stood at his open window and listened, hungering for companionship but at the same time refusing himself the company of others as penance for past wrongdoings only he knew about. At last, when the weary peasants went to sleep and human sounds faded into the silence of the forest, interrupted only by the soft hoo-hoos of hoot owls and the bone-chilling howls of faraway wolves, he sadly closed the shutters, and, absorbed in dark memories, with the friendship of only the crock of red wine in the corner and the flask of vodka under his mattress, he sat by himself in his silent, empty house, suffering in his loneliness.

YEAR after year, season after season, day after day, everything always happened in the same way to the people who lived in the place where nobody stopped.

The woodchoppers always rose at the same time each

day, long before dawn, gathered their axes and saws, disappeared into the Czar's forest, labored from dawn to sunset, then wearily plodded home through the darkness.

The woodchoppers' wives rose each morning even earlier than their husbands. In the blackness before dawn, they kindled a fire and prepared meager breakfasts for their families. All day, they cared for their babies and cleaned house, while their daughters tended the scraggly chickens and skinny goats, weeded the gardens, and searched in the forest for fruits and herbs and mushrooms. And late every afternoon, their daytime work done, the women and girls always spun, sewed, mended, and washed what few clothes these poor people owned.

Even babies were always born in the same season, and when the traveling priest paid his annual visit, they were all baptized at the same time. As they grew up, sons always went to the forest with their fathers to learn to chop down the trees, and daughters stayed home with their mothers, preparing for the time when they, too, would be woodchoppers' wives.

And as the sun rose each day, Yosip the Baker always trudged to the road and, on a stone table sheltered by a small roof, left several large canvas bags of freshly made bread and babkas for the Smolensk-to-Vitebsk stagecoach to pick up. In the afternoon and evening, he always prepared the dough for tomorrow's baking. Each night he listened at the window and then sat alone in his empty house.

It always happened that way, day after day, month after month, year after year, lifetime after lifetime, just as everything always happened in the same way in the place where nobody stopped.

2

EVEN the Czar's soldiers, the cruel and dreaded cossacks, always came at the same time each year—on the third day of the seventh month. On that date the fierce and mustachioed Sergeant Major would ride with his platoon between Vitebsk and Smolensk, seizing recruits to serve in the glorious army of the Czar, searching every village, hamlet, house, cabin and hut, every estate, farm, factory and mill, and scouring the fields, hills, and forests.

It made no difference to the Sergeant Major that some of the men and boys he captured and brutally forced into the Russian army did not want to be soldiers, or had families that would starve in their absence, or were physically unfit, or did not believe in guns and swords and killing and war, or hated the Czar and did not wish to serve him. The Sergeant Major neither understood nor sympathized with such men. He himself had been seized by cossacks when he was a starving fifteen-year-old farm boy. Luckily for him, he had been a rugged youngster and, right away, the life of a soldier had agreed with him. The army became his family. The campground and barracks became his home. The battlefield became his bed.

Warfare became his wife. Russia became his mother, and he thought of the Czar as his father.

He was such a good soldier that after serving for five years as a common private, he was promoted, again and again—to private first class, to corporal, to sergeant, and, finally, after twenty years, to sergeant major.

He considered it a man's principled and principal duty to serve his country without question. Mother Russia had been good to the Sergeant Major. He loved her. Why should not every man love her? It enraged the Sergeant Major when a subject refused to obey her laws. He felt he was doing his duty when he unmercifully punished peasants who defied her. When he disciplined serfs with his whip and sword and boots, in his heart he considered himself a patriot.

SO each year, on the third day of the seventh month, the Sergeant Major would lead his platoon toward the place where nobody stopped. Since Yosip the Baker's house was nearest the road, the cossacks would ride wildly toward his cottage, and, after storming through the nearby woods, and searching behind every tree and under every bush, would thunder up to the front gate, and the Sergeant Major would bellow, "Baker! Baker! Are you here?"

Yosip the Baker would come to the door, wiping the flour from his hands onto his red beard, and greet the barbaric Sergeant Major with a smile, for he wanted company, even if it was a gang of coarse and rowdy soldiers.

"Yes, your Excellency," Yosip would say, "I am here."

Grandly, the Sergeant Major would stand straight up in his stirrups, so that the plume of his silver helmet was as high as the roof of Yosip the Baker's house, and, looking even fiercer than before, take from his saddlebag an important-looking scroll and read (even though he knew it by heart), "In this year of Our Lord eighteen hundred and ninety-five, and in the name of His Most Imperial Czar, Emperor of all the Russias, and of Finland, and of Poland, now hear this! All males between the ages of sixteen and forty-five who are not the eldest son and are sound of limb and senses are herewith commanded, upon penalty of death, to serve in the grand army of His Most Imperial Czar for a period of five years!"

Spreading his arms wide and shrugging his shoulders, Yosip the Baker would always answer, "Your Excellency, all my neighbors are woodchoppers, and they and their sons are exempted from military service because they already work for his Most Imperial Czar in his mighty forest. And I, Yosip, am not eligible to be a soldier for two reasons. I am sixty years of age, so I am too old, and I have already served in the glorious Russian army."

Then Yosip would open his mouth wide and point to a place on his gums where there were no teeth and say, "You see—where a corporal knocked me down with his rifle butt. Before he hit me, I had twenty strong teeth. Afterward I had only ten."

All the soldiers would laugh. The Sergeant Major, whose cruel and evil grin reflected the everyday violence of a warrior's life, would swing his long leg over his horse's neck and leap to the ground, menacingly shake his gloved fist an inch from Yosip the Baker's mouth, and shout above the laughter, "Baker, I'll make a deal with you. If you cook a meal for me and my men, we'll allow you to keep the ten teeth you have left."

While the cossacks laughed even louder, Yosip the Baker would put his hands below his round belly and lift until his chest stuck out, and say, "It is a pleasure and an honor to prepare food for the soldiers of the Czar, and you are welcome in my home," while to himself he would think, "Even the company of a gang of tyrants for two hours a year is better than being alone all the time."

Graciously, he would usher them out of the hot July sun and into the coolness of his house. There, amid the gruff laughter and loud oaths of the cossacks, Yosip the Baker would bake fresh bread and cakes, cook a hearty goat-meat stew, pour red wine from the crock in the corner and vodka from the flask under his mattress, set it all before the hungry cossacks, and watch as they ate, drank, danced their wild dances, and sang martial songs in deep, booming voices. Afterward the soldiers roughly hugged and praised Yosip, telling him what a great baker and extraordinary cook and fine man he was.

So it was that once a year, on the third day of the seventh month, even though the cossacks had never ever captured one single recruit in the place where nobody stopped, they unfailingly came to Yosip the Baker's cottage for a feast, and for that one single afternoon, life and fellowship warmed Yosip the Baker's usually silent and empty house.

It always happened that way, year after year, just as everything always happened the same way in the place where nobody stopped—until, all of a sudden, one year it did not.

3

LONG before dawn one frosty February morning, Yosip the Baker, as always, rose from his iron cot, which hung above the large stone oven to keep him warm during the Russian winter nights, and sleepily dressed.

His eyes still half-closed, he fetched an armful of logs from the neatly stacked woodpile near the cupboard, taking care not to step on or disturb the dozens of unbaked loaves of bread arrayed on clean cloths in every available open space—on the floor, on the big table, on the benches and chairs and windowsills. The afternoon before, Yosip had mixed the dough, added yeast, kneaded and shaped it, and even though he'd been a baker since childhood, he still considered it a wonderment that the loaves, as they sat overnight and breathed while the yeast performed its magic, would rise and expand and transform themselves from small lumps of pasty dough into large, magnificent breads and cakes ready for baking.

Just as he did every morning, he expertly arranged the logs in the brick chamber beneath the oven, lit them, and waited until the fire snapped and blazed. With the instinct of an artist, he watched the fire until it burned exactly the way he wanted. Then Yosip began to slide the unbaked loaves into the oven with a wide wooden spatula. As it baked, the browning bread filled the cottage with incomparably delicious aromas, making Yosip's mouth water and softening his face into a look of pleasure. He enjoyed his work.

When the baking was done, he took the loaves of bread and sweet-smelling babkas from the oven and laid them out to cool on clean cloths upon the floor. Finally, as always, Yosip dropped the finished loaves and cakes into large canvas bags, tied the necks of the bags tightly, and hefted the bulky load onto his shoulders.

What happened next is like a miracle, except that it happened exactly the same way every single morning. Just as he stepped outside to take the bags to the roadside shelter for the stagecoach to pick up, the sun rose. Every morning, the sun always waited for Yosip the Baker to open his door before it poked the top of its head over the horizon.

But this particular morning, just two steps outside the door, Yosip the Baker stopped walking, and this was very strange. Never before had he stopped on the way to the road.

I don't know why he stopped. Even Yosip didn't know. But he felt as if something were going to happen today, something that had never happened before in the place where nobody stopped.

Yosip looked up to see if it was the sky that made him feel this excitement. No, it was just like any other February sky, steely and cold and, on the eastern horizon, tinted pale gold by the weak winter sun.

Perhaps, then, it was the forest, or the woodchoppers' houses, or the muddy road. He looked at the sleeping forest, at his neighbors' shabby dwellings among the trees, at the empty road. No. They were just as they always were. In his mind, Yosip examined his body. Did his back hurt? No. His head, his arms, his legs, his feet? No, no, no, and no.

Shaking his head in befuddlement, he continued toward the road, put the bags in their usual place for the stagecoach to pick up, and returned to his kitchen.

But all day long, as he sifted, measured, mixed, and kneaded, Yosip the Baker felt a strange anticipation fluttering in his round stomach. Why did he feel that this day was different from all other days?

JUST as he was adding yeast to a great lump of dough, the answer came. Yosip the Baker heard the squeal of a cartwheel outside his door.

Wiping the flour from his hands onto his red beard, he stepped through the door and into his yard. Sure enough, there was before him an old oxcart with two great, squeaky, stubborn, wooden wheels mired in the mud.

But the oxcart was being pulled not by an ox, or a horse, or a mule, or even a donkey. Pulling the cart was a tiny man, grunting and straining as hard as he could, a poor, skinny little fellow, his small hands desperately gripping the handles of the cart. He was bent forward so low that his rear end stuck up in the air, his chin almost touched the ground, and the tip of his nose and his black beard and the front brim of his hat dragged in the mud.

Yosip had never seen a more determined person! Oh, how the little man lunged and tugged and jerked. He panted, he gasped, he groaned. He growled, he squawked, he snorted. He mumbled "Oy!" between each breath. He lifted each bony knee all the way up to his shoulder while he dug the other foot deeper into the mud so he could pull harder.

It's too bad that the old cart also had a mind of its own. It moved only a few inches at a time—straight toward Yosip the Baker, who stood just outside his doorway. And because the little man was bent forward and could see only the ground, it looked as if he was going to pull the cart right into Yosip's round stomach and through the very door of the house.

Just as the top of the little man's head was less than an inch from the baker's belly, Yosip said, "Good day, traveler."

Without even looking up, the small man replied, "Good day. Is this the place where nobody stops?" For so tiny a man, the stranger had a deep and melodic voice.

Sadly, Yosip the Baker answered, "Yes. This is the place where nobody stops."

The little man sighed, dropped the handles of the cart, and wearily straightened his bent body. By now, he was standing so close to Yosip the Baker that all he saw was a red beard, while the top of the small man's hat mashed into Yosip's nose, pushing it a little to one side.

Because his nose was pushed to one side, Yosip said in a funny voice, "I am Yosip the Baker. Who are you, my friend?"

"I am Mordecai ben Yahbahbai," answered the short man, but his melodious voice also sounded strange, because his mouth was full of Yosip's beard.

"Greetings, Mordecai ben Yahbahbai. Where do you come from?" asked Yosip the Baker.

"I come from Vitebsk," replied Mordecai ben Yahbahbai.

"Aha," said Yosip the Baker, "and you are on your way to Smolensk."

"No," answered Mordecai ben Yahbahbai, "I am not on my way to Smolensk."

"Oh?" responded Yosip the Baker, with some surprise.

"You said this is the place where nobody stops?" repeated Mordecai ben Yahbahbai.

Yosip tried to shake his head up and down to answer, but as he lowered his chin, his nose pushed Mordecai ben Yahbahbai's hat down over the little man's eyes. Still, Yosip managed to say, "Yes, Mordecai ben Yahbahbai, this is indeed the place where nobody stops."

"Thank God!" exulted Mordecai ben Yahbahbai. "We have finally arrived."

"We?" asked Yosip the Baker. He stepped back from Mordecai ben Yahbahbai and looked around. "We? Who is with you? Who is in the cart?"

"My wife and small daughter are asleep in the cart."

But Mordecai ben Yahbahbai was mistaken. His wife and daughter were not asleep. Over the side of the cart popped two heads, one with a womanly face and shining, intelligent eyes, the other with a child's face, dirty but pretty, with very sleepy eyes.

Yosip the Baker bowed and smiled, but his curiosity

The little man's voice sounded funny because his mouth was full of Yosip's red beard.

quickly made him ask, "Please forgive me for being so personal, but—why do you want to stop *here*? Nobody *ever* stops *here*."

"Nobody ever stops here?" echoed Mordecai ben Yahbahbai's wife, her features becoming very solemn.

"I've lived in this place for twenty-five years, and you're the first travelers who have ever left the road and come to my door."

"Aha!" exclaimed Mordecai ben Yahbahbai, who stuck out his chest like a peacock, put one hand inside his coat, the other hand skyward, and pulled his chin back, thus looking very wise. "And therefore you ask, 'Why are *they*, Mordecai ben Yahbahbai and his wife and daughter, stopping here?' Logic! Logic, my new friend. I am stopping in the place where nobody stops because this is where Shimkeh told me to stop."

"Shimkeh?"

"Yes, Shimkeh," repeated Mordecai ben Yahbahbai, beaming.

After a pause, Yosip the Baker asked, "And—who is Shimkeh?"

"Shimkeh," sighed Mordecai ben Yahbahbai's wife, as if Shimkeh were an evil word.

"Shimkeh," crooned Mordecai ben Yahbahbai, as if Shimkeh were a beautiful word. "Shimkeh is my cousin, who knows many important people in the government. When he heard that my wife, my daughter, and I wanted to go to America, Shimkeh said he would make *all* the arrangements. He told us to come here and wait, and he would bring us passports."

Wearily, Mordecai ben Yahbahbai's wife climbed out of the cart and said to no one in particular, "Shimkeh? Shimkeh? Shimkeh will bring us passports like I'm the wealthiest woman in the Czar's court." She shook her head and declared, "Shimkeh is a liar and a thief. We'll never see Shimkeh or our passports or our life's savings."

With a quiet and understanding smile, as if he had seen his wife sadly shake her head and sigh many times and loved her dearly for it, Mordecai ben Yahbahbai turned to Yosip the Baker and said, "Sometimes my fine wife has no faith in the goodness of humankind. But what are the two things that separate a human being from a beast? Logic and goodness."

Pacing back and forth, waving first one hand, then the other, Mordecai ben Yahbahbai reasoned, "Now what could be more logical than this? Shimkeh, my own dear cousin, my own mother's brother's son, took my life savings, ninety rubles and ten kopecks, and promised that in a short while he would bring passports to me right here, in the place where nobody stops. And this is where logic and goodness enter in: all human beings are good, yes? *Yes!* And Shimkeh is a human being, yes? Therefore, Shimkeh is good. And if Shimkeh is good, I trust him. And if I trust him, I must wait here for him to bring passports, so we can go to America."

Turning to his wife, Mordecai ben Yahbahbai gently said, "What, my love, could be more logical than that?"

Throwing up her hands, Mordecai ben Yahbahbai's wife said to Yosip, "Whenever he talks, he always agrees with himself. That makes two of him against just one of me. So what chance have I against such logic and faith?"

To her husband, she smiled and sighed. "All right, my beloved. As I promised, where you go, I go. Where you stay, I stay. Which means we stay here, in this place, and wait."

Mordecai ben Yahbahbai took his wife's hand and

they nodded fondly at each other, so Yosip the Baker, his thoughts troubled, politely hesitated a moment before he timidly asked, "Er, um, ah, tell me, please—where will you live while you wait for Shimkeh to come with your passports?"

"At the inn, I suppose," answered Mordecai ben Yahbahbai.

Yosip the Baker shook his head. "There is no inn in this place."

"No inn?" Mordecai ben Yahbahbai's eyes grew large and round and his mouth turned downward, like a grown man about to cry.

"No inn?" repeated Mordecai ben Yahbahbai's wife, her eyes also growing large and round and her mouth also turning downward, like a grown woman about to cry.

"Then where *shall* we stay?" whimpered their little daughter, who was still in the cart. And all three of them, Mordecai ben Yahbahbai, his wife and daughter, truly began to cry.

Almost in tears himself, Yosip the Baker put up his hand to stop their tears and said, "Mordecai ben Yahbahbai, I am but a poor tradesman and my house is a humble one. But, for a little while, you and your wife and child may stay with me, if you wish."

As suddenly as a match struck in the dark, Mordecai ben Yahbahbai's tears brightened into a smile. He nodded his head up and down, to show how much he agreed with himself, and explained, "You see? You heard? What did I tell you? All human beings are good. Yosip the Baker, you are a human being. Therefore, Yosip the Baker, you are good."

With his arms lifted heavenward, Mordecai ben Yahbahbai sang out, "Logic, logic, logic. Logic says that if I build a house, and then Shimkeh comes with our passports, the house will be wasted. Why will it be wasted? Because we would go to America, and the house would stay here. So *my* logic and *your* goodness tell me what to do, Yosip the Baker. Thank you, thank you, my new friend. We shall indeed stay with you."

As the two men clasped hands to seal the agreement, Yosip was filled suddenly with new happiness.

Why? Because he knew that for a few days he would no longer be lonely. Beaming, he said, "My new comrades, you are welcome."

4

MORDECAI ben Yahbahbai and his wife, Ginzl, and their six-year-old daughter, Liebeh, unloaded their cart, which was mostly full of books, and moved into Yosip the Baker's small stone house. More cots were hung over the great stone oven so they would all be warm when they slept—and for the household a new life began.

Each dawn Ginzl helped Yosip bake the bread. Each afternoon she helped him mix and knead the dough and shape the loaves they would bake the following morning. She also cooked the most delicious meals Yosip had ever tasted, and, as she worked, she sang in a voice sweeter and richer than the syrup on Yosip the Baker's babkas.

Liebeh was very like her mother. She fed the chickens and gathered their eggs. She helped Ginzl cook and clean. And each dawn, even though her pretty eyes were still half-asleep, she went with Yosip when he carried the bags of bread to the road for the stagecoach to pick up.

Yosip loved little Liebeh from the very first morning, when she asked if she might be his helper. Soon she was adding a half cup of raisins here, a teaspoonful of molasses there, kneading the dough with her lovely child's fingers—while question after question rushed from her busy young mind like water over a steep waterfall. "Why does yeast make bread rise?" "Why is the larder beneath the floor under the trapdoor so much cooler than up in the loft near the roof?" "Why is there a hole in the middle of a babka?" "What is a rainbow?" "Why do I dream?"

Liebeh's questions were unending, and, as Yosip the Baker answered each one, or *tried* to answer each one, his usually expressionless face changed. New and happy lines formed near his mouth from smiling. A starlike twinkle found a permanent home in his eyes.

The only time Liebeh got into trouble, and I, for one, wouldn't call it trouble exactly, was the day she opened one of Mordecai ben Yahbahbai's worn leather valises, took out a few sheets of paper and a pencil, and tried to copy the words in her father's books. When Mordecai ben Yahbahbai saw what she was doing, he said, "Papers and pencils are not for girls. Go play, or help your mama cook." But when she began to cry, her father was so loving and gentle as he held her in his lap, rocked her, and kissed her tears away that, after a few moments of weeping, Liebeh forced the disappointment from her mind and turned her attention to new and more cheerful pursuits. Five minutes later she was outside, running and cavorting with some of her new playmates in the place where nobody stopped.

From the first day Liebeh had arrived, she'd made friends, mostly because a peasant boy named Yuri had appointed himself as her protector and comrade. Four years older than Liebeh, this remarkable ten-year-old lad was tall and muscular for his age, and even though his bright eyes crackled with intelligence and curiosity and sensitivity and good humor, the other boys knew better than to tease him about having girls as playmates. Yes, he seldom raised his voice or became angry, but when it was necessary Yuri could be a very punishing and courageous fighter.

Sooner or later, even without any help, I'm sure Liebeh would have made new friends among the boys and girls of the place where nobody stopped. Thanks to Yuri, however, it wasn't such a hard job. The peasant children, shy and in the beginning very wary of this lovely little stranger from the city, watched Yuri, their leader, come forward and welcome her, and saw that within minutes the twinkling stranger and Yuri liked and respected each other.

"I am Yuri," he said gently, "son of Gregor and nephew of Oleg, the strongest and wisest woodchopper in the Czar's forest."

"My name is Liebeh," she answered. Trying to speak as Yuri had, she added, "Daughter of Ginzl and Mordecai ben Yahbahbai—and I'm happy to know you, Yuri, son of Gregor and nephew of Oleg." She smiled at him and did what she did so often—she set him at ease with a barrage of questions which were easy for him to answer and therefore made him feel comfortable as he spoke with her.

Looking at his waist, she asked, "Is that your own knife? Aren't you afraid, having such a big knife hanging from your belt? What is the beautiful handle made of?"

Hesitating for only a second—peasant children did not speak as quickly or as readily as Liebeh—he answered, "Yes, this is my own knife. It was given to me by my father when I reached the age of ten and someday when I have my first son I shall give it to him when he is ten. My uncle says the handle is made of the horn of a mighty moose whose antlers reached higher than a house when he lived."

Impressed, Liebeh said, "Oh, my! What do you use the knife for?"

This question, whose answer was so obvious to Yuri, puzzled him and made him hesitate longer than a second. Finally, studying Liebeh's face closely to make sure she wasn't making fun of him, he replied, "I use my knife for cutting."

Her laugh echoed like sweet chimes. "I know *that*. But for cutting *what*?"

"Many things. Rope, wood, meat, potatoes. When I search for mushrooms in the forest and find a large clump, my knife cuts their stems."

"Mushrooms come from the forest? *This* forest?" she exclaimed. Fascinated with her, Yuri studied the way Liebeh's face radiated with delight when she learned something new. "The only mushrooms I ever saw were in the bazaar."

"Bazaar?" he asked, without changing his intent expression. "What is a bazaar?"

"A huge place where there are many stalls full of things to buy and wagons full of fruits and vegetables. The busiest place in the city."

"The city?" he whispered. Liebeh could tell by his faraway look that the very idea of the city awed and mystified Yuri. "Tell me about the city," he said.

Liebeh answered him with her most impish smile. "Very well—if you'll tell me about the forest."

He smiled. Liebeh thought it was the most beautiful smile she'd ever seen.

"A fair deal," he said, spitting in his right palm and extending his hand toward Liebeh.

She was uncertain about what to do for only a moment. Then, elated with her new friend and the bargain she was about to seal, she also spat on the palm of her hand and held it out.

Smiling at each other, Liebeh and Yuri shook hands, this city girl whose forebears were scholars, this peasant boy whose ancestors were serfs, and their friendship took root as surely as a shiny, tiny acorn on the forest floor is destined to grow one day into a strong and beautiful oak.

AND what about Mordecai ben Yahbahbai?

Did he, too, make new friends? If ever there was a question whose answer was yes, this is that question. Yes, indeed, Mordecai ben Yahbahbai made many new friends.

On his first day in the place where nobody stopped, he took a walk and had a discussion with the grandmother of the woodchopper who lived closest to Yosip the Baker.

On the second day, he took a walk and had a discussion with the one-armed great-uncle of the woodchopper who lived just beyond the grandmother of the first woodchopper.

On the third day, he took a walk and had a discussion with the aunt and niece of the woodchopper who lived just beyond the woodchopper's one-armed great-uncle who lived just beyond the woodchopper's grandmother who lived closest to Yosip the Baker.

And so on, and so on. Every day, Mordecai ben Yahbahbai took a walk. Every day, he had a discussion with a different neighbor.

And soon he was looked upon by the folk of the place where nobody stopped as the most wonderful man in the world.

You ask, "Why?"

All right, I'll tell you.

The woodchoppers and their families were simple, uneducated people. The only place the men ever went was to the Czar's forest, where they toiled from daybreak to nightfall. The women lived even narrower lives. They slaved as hard as the men, rearing and feeding and nursing their families, and almost never left the place where nobody stopped.

The only people from the outside world whom these serfs ever saw were a priest and a peddler. The priest passed through once every year and stayed just long enough to bless and baptize the newborn babies, as I've told you, and marry young couples and say a prayer for the souls of those who had died. The peddler came more often, every six months or so, and sold pots, pans, axes, saws, needles, thread, and cloth from his rickety wagon. Otherwise, the woodchoppers and their families lived in isolation.

And then came Mordecai ben Yahbahbai, storyteller of storytellers. Suddenly, a light blazed and lit up the darkness, drove away ignorance, and brought forth new and fascinating worlds.

Every night, the woodchoppers and their families gathered in Yosip the Baker's stone cottage to listen to Mordecai ben Yahbahbai's tales, and with his words he freed them from the place where nobody stopped.

Outside, the Russian nights were dark and empty, but inside Yosip the Baker's house, Mordecai ben Yahbahbai made the room warm and full of miracles. From Yuri's sunny and eager young face to Uncle Oleg's craggy and furrowed and thoughtful countenance to the wrinkled features of the oldest grandmother, all sat mesmerized, alert, shiny-eyed, on benches, milking stools, chairs, the floor, the table, windowsills, spellbound by the magic of Mordecai ben Yahbahbai's eloquence.

And when one of his audience—Yuri, quite often—asked him a question born of a lack of education, such as, "When Magellan sailed around the earth and reached the other side of the world, his ship would be upside-down, yes? So why didn't Magellan and his sailors fall off?" Mordecai ben Yahbahbai reached deep down into his powers as a teacher and explained and explained, until every head in the room nodded in comprehension.

Later, after the storytelling, Mordecai ben Yahbahbai played his balalaika and made up rhymes, and suddenly the music and words became a song. Meanwhile, Ginzl began to sing along with him, at first softly, then even more beautifully than her husband. Later, little Liebeh accompanied her parents, her delicate soprano voice as true as a silver bell.

Finally, the peasants and their families joined in, especially Yuri, his high-pitched boyish tenor rich and pure, and Uncle Oleg, whose bass tones were deep and strong. By the end of the evening, everyone was laughing and dancing, grandmothers with grandfathers, husbands

---

After the storytelling, Mordecai ben Yahbahbai played his balalaika and made up rhymes. . . .

with wives, children with children, and blushing maidens with shy young men—all because of Mordecai ben Yahbahbai.

FOR the next four months, Ginzl, Liebeh, and Mordecai ben Yahbahbai were guests in Yosip the Baker's house. And, as if nothing had happened in the place where nobody stopped, once again everything began to happen the same way.

Before dawn, Yosip and Ginzl would bake the bread and put it in bags, Liebeh and Yosip would open the door, the sun would rise, the two of them would carry the bags to the roadside shelter for the stagecoach to pick up, and Yosip would go back into the house.

But Liebeh always remained at the side of the road. Clambering to the top of the shelter's low roof, she would stand for five minutes looking toward Vitebsk, squinting her eyes as hard as she could in order to see further. But the road was always empty, and she would jump to the ground, run into the house, and shout, "Papa! Papa!"

Mordecai ben Yahbahbai, snuffling and snorting, would waken from a deep sleep. He always stayed in bed until noon, since storytelling and singing were hard work.

Rubbing his eyes and trying to raise his head, he would mumble, "Yes? What is it, my sweet Liebehle?"

"Papa! Papa!" she would say. "I looked toward Vitebsk, and guess what I saw? Nothing. The road is empty. Shimkeh is not coming with our passports."

Ginzl, not even looking up from her cooking, would

smile a rueful smile and sigh, "Shimkeh? Shimkeh will come with our passports like I'm the wealthiest lady in the Czar's court. Shimkeh? Oh, that liar. That thief."

But Mordecai ben Yahbahbai, snuggling further down into the warm cot, would mumble, "Logic, my loving Ginzl. Human beings are good. Shimkeh is a human being. Therefore, Shimkeh is good." Yawning, his mumbling fading into snores, he would add, "Therefore, I trust him. He'll come. Passports. America. You'll see, you'll see."

And in less than a second, he would fall back into a deep and sweet sleep, so that in the afternoon he would be rested enough to take walks, visit neighbors, have discussions, read books, write poems, and, when evening came, have the energy he needed to tell stories and sing songs.

5

AND then came the third day of the seventh month, and Yosip the Baker, engrossed in his new life, forgot that it was always on this day that the cossacks scoured the forests and hamlets for recruits for the Czar's glorious army.

It was a golden summer afternoon. As Yosip the Baker and Ginzl kneaded dough for tomorrow's bread, Mordecai ben Yahbahbai sat by the window, reading and thinking.

Outside, Liebeh and Yuri fed bread crumbs to a pair of chipmunks, a tortoise, and a host of sparrows. Because Yuri towered above the other children, his family sometimes forgot he was only ten and treated him like a fully grown man, giving him double the chores a boy his age normally would have. He never complained and did his work, chopping firewood, repairing the thatched roof, cleaning the chimney, carrying, fixing, digging, hammering, helping the cow or goat give birth, scaring off the foxes who threatened the chicken coop, supervising the other children when they gathered berries in the forest. Since Liebeh's entrance into his life, however, he worked twice as hard and twice as fast, so that each afternoon he always had an hour or so to spend with her.

But on this particular afternoon, the third day of the seventh month, as Liebeh and Yuri fed the tiny animals, they felt the earth tremble and heard a distant rumbling, the thunder of many horses' hooves, and the clanking and jangling of steel spurs and heavy swords. Panicked, the sparrows flew away, the chipmunks fled toward the forest, the tortoise withdrew into its shell. Yuri stood up. Peering into the distance, his eyes wide but his voice calm, he said to Liebeh, "Cossacks."

"Cossacks?" echoed Liebeh.

"Terrible men who steal from the poor and burn our houses and kill innocent people. I hate them."

"Oh, my," whispered Liebeh.

"I have to go home now. My mama and sisters are alone and need me to protect them. Go into the house, Liebeh," he said, his voice showing no fear. Quickly, he was gone, running toward his own cabin.

Liebeh stood up and stared at the road. Far along it, a cloud of dust from the cossacks' galloping horses came nearer and nearer. Afraid, she ran into the house, shouting, "Papa! Mama! Yosip! Cossacks are coming! Soldiers with shiny swords and tall plumes on their helmets! On big, black horses!"

"Oh, my God, no!" gasped Yosip the Baker.

Mordecai ben Yahbahbai and Ginzl did not seem too disturbed that soldiers were riding by, but Yosip the Baker remembered suddenly what day of the year it was and why the soldiers were coming.

Solemnly, he put his hand on Mordecai ben Yahbahbai's shoulder and asked, "My good friend, how old are you?"

Mordecai ben Yahbahbai was puzzled by the question, but he answered his friend, "I was born the year before Czar Alexander the Second, of the house of Romanov, grandfather of Czar Alexander the Third, of the house of Romanov, and father of the glorious Czar Nicholas the Second, also of the house of Romanov—"

"My dear Mordecai ben Yahbahbai," stammered Yosip the Baker, "please tell me, quickly! How old are you?"

"As I was trying to tell you, dear Yosip the Baker," explained Mordecai ben Yahbahbai, "I was born the year before Czar Alexander the Second, of the house of Romanov, freed the serfs."

Trying to stay calm, Yosip the Baker asked, "And what year was that, my friend?"

"Eighteen sixty."

"Eighteen sixty—and this is eighteen ninety-six."

"Which makes me thirty-six years of age."

"Oh, no!" moaned Yosip the Baker.

"Thirty-six is not good? What can I do about it? I had no control over when I was born."

"Unfortunately, that's true."

Yosip the Baker wrung his hands, paced, thought, then brightened a bit. "Are you the eldest son in your family?"

"Oh, no," laughed Mordecai ben Yahbahbai. "I am the youngest son in a family of eleven brothers."

Becoming more distressed each moment, Yosip the Baker asked, "And are you sound of limb and senses?"

Making a ropy muscle with his skinny arm, Mordecai ben Yahbahbai proclaimed, "As sound as a man can be, thank God." Cocking his head to the left and to the right, like a rooster trying to get a better look at a fox, Mordecai ben Yahbahbai inquired of Yosip the Baker, "Why are you asking me all this, my friend?"

But Ginzl, who was smarter and wiser than her husband in many ways, by now knew very well why Yosip the Baker was upset.

"Let Yosip ask the questions, my love," she instructed Mordecai ben Yahbahbai, "and you answer."

"Whatever you say, my beautiful wife. Ask, then, Yosip. Ask. I will answer," smiled Mordecai ben Yahbahbai.

"I have just one more question," groaned Yosip the Baker. Not really wanting to hear the response, he cleared his throat, held on to his apron for support, and asked, "Mordecai ben Yahbahbai, have you ever served in the army of the Czar?"

"The army of the Czar? Ho, ho. Ha, ha. Me? In the army? *Never!*" laughed Mordecai ben Yahbahbai.

But as he saw the horror in Yosip the Baker's eyes and desperation in Ginzl's face, suddenly Mordecai ben Yahbahbai realized why the soldiers were coming. His laughter instantly froze into a look of terror.

"Oh, no!" he wailed. "They're coming to take *me*? *Me* they're coming to take?"

Looking heavenward, Mordecai ben Yahbahbai screamed, "Where is the logic of this? If I'm in the Czar's army, how can I go to America? Oy, what shall I do? Yosip the Baker, Ginzl, *help*! You're a good man, Yosip. Therefore, you *must* help! *Please*, my friend!"

The thunder from the soldiers' horses was now so near, the house began to shake. The crock in the corner danced. The door of the great stone oven rattled and the iron cots vibrated.

Yosip the Baker ran to the window, praying the horsemen would ride by, that just this once they would not stop in the place where nobody stopped. But no! The mounted men turned off the road, stormed through the woods surrounding the cottage, searching behind every tree and under every bush, then cantered straight toward Yosip the Baker's house.

"Oh, me! Oh, my!" whispered Yosip the Baker. To stop his hands from shaking, he stroked his red beard with rapid little tugs, like a chicken-plucker at work.

Desperately, he looked around his one-room house for a place to hide Mordecai ben Yahbahbai, Ginzl, and Liebeh. But where? Behind the crock in the corner? No. The crock was too small because Ginzl was too tall. Under the table? No. It was too easy to see someone hiding under the table. Then where? *Where?*

His heart beating faster than the pounding of the oncoming horses' hooves, Yosip the Baker's brain whirled so violently that perspiration dripped down his nose and into his beard.

Outside the house, the thunder stopped. Like the call of The Angel of Death, the Sergeant Major's deep voice boomed, "Baker! Baker! Are you here?"

And just as it seemed that Mordecai ben Yahbahbai was doomed, Yosip the Baker thought of a hiding place.

"Quickly, quickly, *into the flour barrel*!" hissed Yosip the Baker to Mordecai ben Yahbahbai, who was crying and stuffing the end of his black beard into his mouth to keep from making a sound.

"The flour barrel?" blubbered Mordecai ben Yahbahbai, as Yosip the Baker lifted the heavy, round, wooden lid off the large container.

"Baker! Baker! Are you here?" the Sergeant Major shouted again, this time more harshly.

"Yes, the flour barrel!" growled Yosip the Baker, unhappily. Seizing the seat of Mordecai ben Yahbahbai's trousers with one hand and the back of his collar with the other, in one powerful heave Yosip lifted the little man up in the air and stuffed him, feet first, into the flour barrel.

"Crouch down, so I can put the lid on," commanded Yosip in a desperate whisper.

"But, but, but—Yosip," wept Mordecai ben Yahbahbai, "suppose the flour gets in my nose and I sneeze?"

"Do you want to serve the next five years in the Czar's army?" Yosip asked.

"No," sobbed Mordecai ben Yahbahbai.

"Then I advise you not to sneeze," said Yosip through gritted teeth.

After the briefest of pauses, Mordecai ben Yahbahbai whimpered, "That's good advice. I won't sneeze."

Reluctantly, slowly, he crouched down until only his eyes and the very top of his head remained in view, but as Yosip impatiently replaced the heavy lid on the flour barrel, it accidentally bumped the top of Mordecai ben Yahbahbai's head.

"Ouch!" wept Mordecai ben Yahbahbai from inside the barrel.

Lifting the lid a crack and peering into the big container, Yosip the Baker whispered, "Are you all right? It was an accident. Please excuse me."

"I'm all right. You're excuse-soo-soo-saa-aaaahh-aa-aahhhh-chooooh!" replied Mordecai ben Yahbahbai.

"God bless you," sighed Yosip the Baker. This time,

as Yosip again closed the lid, Mordecai ben Yahbahbai crouched low enough to keep his head out of danger. At last he was out of sight. But from inside the barrel, his voice muffled, he said, "Don't worry. I won't aah-aah-aah-hmm-hmm sneeze again."

Meanwhile, Ginzl, clearer of mind and braver than any of them, hid Liebeh in the sugar keg and closed the top. Lastly, she knelt and opened the bottom of the cupboard, but as she began to climb inside, headfirst, her hips became stuck in the doorway.

"Push!" she whispered to Yosip the Baker.

"Me? Push?" he answered.

"Do you see anyone else here? Yes, you, Yosip. Do you think God Almighty is going to send an angel to put his hands on my rear and get me unstuck? Push, Yosip! Push!"

Yosip the Baker closed his eyes, looked away, put his hands behind Ginzl, took a deep breath, and gave her a mighty shove. With a whoosh, she became unstuck and tumbled into the bottom of the cupboard. Quickly, Yosip closed and bolted the cupboard door.

"Blast you, Baker! Where are you?" roared the Sergeant Major from outside. "Do you hear me, you swine? Are you here?"

Yosip the Baker looked upward in prayer before facing the cossacks. Trembling inwardly, he stepped out of his house and into the yard, and said to the Sergeant Major, in the calmest voice he could manage, "Yes, your Excellency, I am here."

"Then why did you not answer the first time I hailed you?" growled the Sergeant Major, his waxed mustache quivering in rage.

"I am getting old, your Excellency," said Yosip the

Baker, trying to smile, even though his round belly quaked and shivered with fright. "My ears are not as sharp as they once were. Please forgive me if I did not hear you." Yosip the Baker had never lied before, and not telling the Sergeant Major the truth was very difficult for him.

"Humph," snorted the Sergeant Major. "Your ears, eh?" Slowly, the anger fled his fierce face. "Your ears, eh?" he repeated. Turning to his men and winking, he said to Yosip the Baker, "Maybe there's dough in your ears."

"Ha, ha, ha!" roared his soldiers. Yosip the Baker, relieved, laughed with them.

"Maybe," continued the Sergeant Major, "there's as much dough in your ears as there is *in a barrel of flour*!"

"Ho, ho, ho!" roared the soldiers again.

Yosip the Baker, horrified at the mention of the flour barrel, stammered, "Yes, yes, you are right, your Eminence. There are no ears in my dough. I mean, uh, um, there is nothing in my dough, except for the barrels in my ears. I mean—oh, me! Oh, my!" Yosip the Baker was a very bad liar.

The soldiers laughed even louder as Yosip the Baker, stuttering and sputtering, wrung his red beard in dismay, until the Sergeant Major shouted, "Enough!"

No longer smiling and looking fiercer than ever, the Sergeant Major stood straight up in his stirrups so that the plume of his shiny helmet was as high as the roof of Yosip the Baker's house. Grandly, he took the important-looking scroll from his saddlebag, unrolled it, and began to read (even though he knew it by heart), "In this year of Our Lord eighteen hundred and ninety-six, and in the name of His Most Imperial Czar, Emperor of All the Russias, and of Finland, and of Poland, now hear this!

All males between the ages of sixteen and forty-five who are not the eldest son and are sound of limb and senses are herewith commanded, upon the penalty of death, to serve in the grand army of the Czar for a period of five years!"

His face feverish and mouth dry, Yosip the Baker flicked out his tongue again and again to moisten his parched lips. When he answered, he could hardly swallow and his words came out in a froglike croak.

"Your Excellency," rasped Yosip the Baker, "except for the Czar's woodchoppers, I am the only mule, uh, male here, and I have already Czarred on the glorious farm, uh, served in the glorious army of the Czar." He opened his mouth and pointed to the place on his gums where there were no teeth. "You see where a corporal knocked me down with his rifle butt. Before he hit me I had twenty sweet throngs, uh, twenty strong teeth. Afterward, I had only ten."

As always, the soldiers guffawed, the Sergeant Major swung his long leg over his horse's neck, leaped to the ground, shook his gloved fist an inch from Yosip the Baker's mouth, and shouted above the men's laughter, "Baker, I'll make you a promise. If you cook us a meal, we'll allow you to keep the ten teeth you have left."

But for the very first time, Yosip the Baker did *not* say, "It will be a pleasure and honor to serve the soldiers of the Czar."

Haltingly, trying to control his shaking lips and summoning all his courage, Yosip the Baker said hoarsely, "May it please your most gracious Magnificence, I must go into my house and see if there is any food."

Yosip the Baker heard grumbles of displeasure from among the cossacks. The Sergeant Major stared at him in cold silence for a moment, then stepped back and growled ominously, "As you wish, Baker. Go and see if there is food in your house."

To his men the Sergeant Major said through clenched jaws, "Why must these peasants force me to teach them such hard lessons? I do not wish to hurt anyone, but they forget—I represent the Czar of All the Russias!" Bellowing at Yosip the Baker, he roared, "Very well, dog! Insult me and you insult the Czar! Go see if there is food! And remember my promise. If you feed my men, I shall allow you to keep the teeth you have left!"

From his saddle he unstrapped a thick, braided riding crop of shiny black leather. Smacking the heavy crop into his hand with loud thwacks, he roared, "Go, then! See if there is food!" Glaring, he jabbed the end of the crop into poor Yosip the Baker's chest and roughly pushed him.

On stiff legs numb with fright, Yosip the Baker hurried into his house. He stopped at the window to make sure the cossacks were not peeping in, then went to the flour barrel and whispered, "Mordecai ben Yahbahbai, can you hear me?"

"He can hear you," came Ginzl's voice, from inside the cupboard.

"Shhhhhh! Not so loud," whispered Yosip the Baker. Watching the window, he said softly to the flour barrel, "The soldiers want me to bake for them, Mordecai ben Yahbahbai. What should I do?"

For a moment there was silence. Then, again from inside the cupboard, Ginzl answered. "Mordecai ben Yahbahbai says to use logic. If my husband is in the flour barrel, and if you bake the cossacks a meal, the meal will be Mordecai ben Yahbahbai."

"On the other hand," moaned Yosip the Baker to himself, "if I do *not* bake for the cossacks . . ." He thought of the Sergeant Major's enraged face and the thick, braided riding crop of shiny black leather. And he thought of the ten teeth he had left and wanted very much to keep.

Like a condemned man on his way to the whipping post, Yosip the Baker walked through the door of his house and back into the yard, his eyes on the ground.

"Well? Well? Is there food in the house, Baker?" barked the Sergeant Major. "Speak up, Baker. Speak up!"

Yosip's trembling lips tried to form words, but no sounds came from his mouth. Wheezing and hissing, he managed to say, "Uh, n-no f-food-d-d in th-th-the h-h-house, your Exce-exce-excelen-suh-suh-cy."

The Sergeant Major's eyes blazed red with fury. Yosip the Baker was sure that tongues of fire would shoot out of them and, in one terrible bolt of flame, turn him into smoldering ashes.

Instead, the Sergeant Major raised his heavy, braided riding crop. Shouting, "Selfish peasant! Now you will see that I keep my promises," he struck Yosip the Baker again and again, beating him on the head, the shoulders, the elbows, the face, the back and seat and belly and ears and everywhere—until Yosip the Baker fell to the ground, nearly unconscious.

As his men cheered and roared their approval, the Sergeant Major stood over Yosip the Baker and began to kick him with his shiny black boots. Oh, how it hurt! The boots' pointed toes dug into his ribs, the sharp heels ground into his back, the steely spurs cut his clothes and slashed his arms and legs.

Dimly, through bitter pain, Yosip the Baker was aware of the men cursing, whistling, laughing, and shouting high above him, and their horses snorting, sniffing, whinnying, and pawing the ground next to his fallen body. Above it all, the Sergeant Major screamed, "Greedy Baker! Selfish peasant! This will teach you respect for the soldiers of the Czar! Tightfisted bumpkin! Ignorant swine!"

Finally, the Sergeant Major wearied of kicking Yosip the Baker. Still furious, he mounted his horse and looked down at the poor man, curled up in the dirt below his horse's feet, and bellowed, "Am I not a man of my word? Do I not keep my promises? Look *now*, Baker, and see if you still have ten teeth!"

Shaking the earth, the cossacks' horses wheeled around and around the yard, kicking clods of dirt into Yosip the Baker's battered, swollen, bloodied face, until the Sergeant Major cried, "Forward!" The soldiers reined their horses into a line, galloped toward the road, and sped away from the place where nobody stopped.

When the thunder of their hooves was gone, Yosip the Baker opened his eyes. He knew his head and face were bloody and every inch of his body bruised.

But for the moment, as he huddled there in the mud, he was aware of only one thing. Just in front of his eyes, gleaming in the dark dirt, lay one of his strong, white teeth.

Although it hurt him to move, Yosip the Baker slowly raised his arm, felt inside his mouth with his finger, and counted his teeth. One. Two. Three. Four. Five. Six. Seven. Eight. Nine.

Nine teeth left.

Groaning, Yosip the Baker managed to get to his feet.

He stumbled into his house and heaved the lid off the flour barrel. Slowly, Mordecai ben Yahbahbai's head appeared, his flour-covered beard and face ghostly white.

Through cracked and bleeding lips Yosip the Baker rasped, "You may sneeze now. The cossacks have gone."

For one of the few times in his life, Mordecai ben Yahbahbai was speechless. Tears ran down his face and made rivers through the flour as he watched Yosip struggle across the room, lift the top off the sugar keg and help Liebeh out, and unbolt the bottom door of the cupboard, releasing Ginzl.

"Oh, my God!" she wept as soon as she saw Yosip's bloody face. To Mordecai ben Yahbahbai she wailed, "See what they've done to him! Mordecai, do something! Say something!"

Mordecai ben Yahbahbai opened his mouth to speak, but all that came out was, "Aaahhhhh-chooooh!"

"Mordecai," wailed Ginzl at the sight of Yosip's bleeding face. "Say something!"

6

GINZL, sobbing, doctored Yosip the Baker's wounds, while Mordecai ben Yahbahbai paced around and around him, crying again and again, "Have you ever seen such goodness? Nurse him tenderly, my Ginzl. Yosip the Baker, you have saved us. Saved us with your selfless courage. Never has there been such a valiant man."

Yosip the Baker sat on a stool. Ginzl gently rubbed liniment on his punished muscles and applied salve to his burning cuts.

"Wipe the flour off your face, Mordecai," breathed Yosip. "You look like a skinny snowman."

Liebeh, her big eyes round and solemn, held Yosip the Baker's hand and put her beautiful head on his shoulder. If he grimaced or groaned as Ginzl nursed his wounds, the child stood on her tiptoes and tried to kiss away the sorrow from his cheek.

Later, the woodchoppers and their families came. In honor of Yosip the Baker's heroism, Mordecai ben Yahbahbai composed a song in which Yosip the Baker drove away the soldiers after a fierce battle. Into the night, they all sang the song again and again.

After the woodchoppers and their families went home, Mordecai ben Yahbahbai, Ginzl, and Liebeh helped poor Yosip climb into his cot.

"Your song about me was untrue, but I enjoyed it anyway and I thank you," the baker managed to say. Talking pained his mouth, his throat, his chest.

"Look who says thank you," responded Mordecai ben Yahbahbai. "It is we who are forever in your debt."

"Sleep, dear Yosip," murmured Ginzl.

"Dream sweetly," said Liebeh, kissing his hand. "Forget those mean and terrible soldiers."

"Yes, yes, yes," he replied. "I shall sleep. I shall dream. Good-night."

But Yosip the Baker did not sleep. Long after the others went to bed, he lay awake on his cot above the great stone oven.

Silence filled the cottage, except for Mordecai ben Yahbahbai's snores and snuffles, Ginzl's occasional low sighs, and Liebeh's soft and regular breathing as she nestled in the blissfully deep and healing sleep of a child.

The summer moon stared one-eyed through the window. Blinking away tears of pain, Yosip the Baker stared back. His body was so sore it hurt him to breathe. His head ached. The inside of his mouth was torn and throbbing. A million jumbled thoughts played hide-and-seek inside his whirling head.

"Tomorrow I shall have a talk with Mordecai ben Yahbahbai," thought Yosip the Baker. "I shall look very stern and say to him, 'My friend, you have been in my house for over four months, and Shimkeh has not come with your passports. Today, *this minute*, you must go to Vitebsk, find Shimkeh, and make him give you your passports!'

"That is what I must do," thought Yosip the Baker. "Then Mordecai ben Yahbahbai will be ashamed of himself and say to me, 'You are right! I am leaving *right this minute*! Because logic tells me that if Shimkeh is in *Vitebsk* and I am *here*, then either I must go to Vitebsk to see Shimkeh, or Shimkeh must come here to see me. But Shimkeh will *never* come here. Ginzl is right. Shimkeh is a liar and a thief. He tricked me. He took my life's savings and then sent me to a place where nobody stops, especially Shimkeh! Therefore, since Shimkeh will never come here, I must go to him. Good-bye, Yosip the Baker. Good-bye, Ginzl. Good-bye, Liebehle. I'm leaving for Vitebsk *this minute* to find Shimkeh!' "

His problem solved, Yosip the Baker smiled at the moon, even though it hurt his face to do it, closed his eyes contentedly, and was almost asleep—when suddenly his eyes again opened wide.

"Suppose he refuses to go," thought Yosip the Baker. "Suppose Mordecai ben Yahbahbai becomes angry and says, 'Logic. Logic, Baker. If I go looking for Shimkeh in Vitebsk, while I am there he may come here looking for me. Therefore, why should I go to Vitebsk if Shimkeh is not there? Be logical, foolish Baker.'

"Or," thought Yosip the Baker, "Mordecai ben Yahbahbai might compose another song about me on his balalaika, a song telling how brave and loyal and good I am, a song about me that all my neighbors will sing. How can I be stern with a trusting, vulnerable, and helpless poet and scholar whose heart is full of love for me?

"Or," thought Yosip the Baker, "suppose Mordecai ben Yahbahbai whines and cries and gets down on his knees and wails, 'But the road is too dusty in the summer, and I might choke to death. Instead, I will go in the fall.

But in the fall the road is covered with leaves and I might get lost. So I will go in the winter—except that in the winter the road is icy; I might slip and break my neck and die like a frozen dog in the middle of a snowdrift. So I will go in the spring, when the road is muddy and flooded with rain, even though I will most surely catch cold, or drown. But if you want me to choke or get lost or break my neck or drown—'

"Oh, no!" thought Yosip the Baker. "Mordecai ben Yahbahbai will never go! Never!"

Yosip the Baker put his hands over his bruised ears, trying to quiet his fevered thoughts. But his mind was made up. Determined, he clenched his teeth—only nine left now, and every one hurting—and said to himself, "Stop! Stop! No more excuses, Mordecai ben Yahbahbai! No more logic! Tomorrow, either you leave to find Shimkeh, or I'll pick you up by the neck and *throw* you all the way to Vitebsk; then you won't need the road because you'll be flying through the air! Tomorrow, for sure! Why should I be beaten by the Sergeant Major because your cousin Shimkeh is a liar and a thief?"

The problem resolved, once again Yosip the Baker closed his eyes to sleep.

And once again, just as he was about to tumble into unconsciousness, a final, terrible thought came to him.

What if Mordecai ben Yahbahbai *does* go to Vitebsk? What if he *finds* Shimkeh and comes back proudly waving the passports over his head? What then?

"Oh, me. Oh, my," thought Yosip the Baker. It would mean that Mordecai ben Yahbahbai, Ginzl, and precious little Liebeh would *leave* the place where nobody stopped. They would go to America.

And Yosip the Baker would be alone again, with no

one to talk to but himself, with no companionship except for the great stone oven, the crock of red wine in the corner, and the flask of vodka under his mattress. Once more, he would be a lonely old man in an empty, silent house.

When he finally fell asleep, Yosip the Baker had a nightmare. The great stone oven opened its iron door wide so that it looked like the Sergeant Major's cruel mouth and began to sing a song that mocked Yosip. The crock in the corner began to dance like a cossack and gurgle and laugh at him. Every time he reached for the flask of vodka, it changed its shape to a riding crop and struck him across the face. He tried to run outside, to escape the mocking and laughing and beating. But there were no windows, no doors, no chimney, no way to leave his house. It was a tomb. He was alone, a prisoner in an empty house, forever!

All the while, the oven sang, in a belching voice that sounded like the Sergeant Major's, "Selfish old Baker, heart of stone; you threw your friends out, now suffer—alone."

Shivering, he awoke from his nightmare. What to do, what to do? His body aching, his heart breaking, his thoughts burning and churning inside his tortured head, Yosip the Baker moaned and groaned the whole night through.

AS always, the next morning long before dawn Yosip the Baker rose from his tortured dreams and he and Ginzl began their daily work. It wasn't easy for him, crouching as he kindled the fire, stooping to pick up the loaves, painfully carrying them one at a time across the room and sliding them into the oven, but he somehow managed to ignore his wounds, and soon the delicious fragrance of baking bread perfumed the cottage.

Just as the sun came out, he and Liebeh stepped from the door and took the bags to the roadside for the stage-coach to pick up. Yosip the Baker limped back into the house. Liebeh stared toward Vitebsk for five minutes and ran back after him, shouting, "Papa! Papa! Shimkeh is not coming with the passports." Ginzl sighed, "Shimkeh? Shimkeh is a liar and a thief." Mordecai ben Yahbahbai opened one eye and mumbled, "Shimkeh is good. He will come with the passports, you'll see," and then went back to sleep.

All morning, Yosip the Baker practiced to himself what he would say to Mordecai ben Yahbahbai when he awoke. "You *must*! I *insist*! *No* excuses! *No* logic! *No* alibis! *No* crying! *No* begging! Just *go*! *Now*!" Every time Mordecai ben Yahbahbai rolled over in his sleep and looked as if he were about to waken, Yosip the Baker limped to the cot and stood and waited, sometimes saying, softly, "Mordecai ben Yahbahbai, can you hear me?" But the only answers were snores and snorts, sniffles and snuffles, whistles and wheezes. As Ginzl put fresh dressings on his burning wounds, Yosip watched Mordecai ben Yahbahbai intently, but the little man hardly stirred.

Finally, Mordecai ben Yahbahbai wakened, rolled over, and saw Yosip the Baker standing next to his cot.

"Aha, Yosip, my friend," yawned Mordecai ben Yahbahbai. "Good morning. How did you know I wanted to talk to you?"

"*You* wanted to talk to *me*?" said Yosip the Baker.

"Absolutely," answered Mordecai ben Yahbahbai, sitting up and hanging his skinny legs over the side of the cot. "I wanted to talk to you yesterday, but something terrible happened. What was it? Oh, yes, I remember now. The soldiers came."

Feeling with the tip of his tongue inside his mouth where tooth number ten had been, Yosip the Baker said, "Yes, the soldiers came." With determination he added, "And I want to talk to *you*, Mordecai ben Yahbahbai."

"First, me," laughed Mordecai ben Yahbahbai, jumping from his cot to the floor and putting each of his hands on Yosip the Baker's shoulders. "First, me, because *my* news is so wonderful that if I do not tell you immediately, I shall explode! And logic tells me that since you are a good man, you do not want me to explode."

Right away, the conversation was not proceeding the way Yosip the Baker had planned it. As he sighed, his ribs ached where the Sergeant Major's boot had left him black and blue, but he managed to say, "Yes. Don't explode. What is your news, Mordecai ben Yahbahbai?"

"Simply this," beamed Mordecai ben Yahbahbai. He took one of Yosip the Baker's cheeks between his thumb and index finger, and, with each word, pinched harder and harder with joy. "You, dear Yosip the Baker, are going to have—a *visitor*!"

"Please. My face. It is injured. Don't pinch so hard." Suddenly, Yosip the Baker realized what he had just heard and stared in amazement. "What did you say? Another visitor? But I already have *three* visitors."

"And now," rhapsodized Mordecai ben Yahbahbai, beginning to pinch Yosip the Baker's other cheek as well, but very, very gently, "and now you are going to have *another* visitor!" Breaking into a happy yai-dai-dai-dai-dai melody, he danced around the room, singing, "A *little* visitor! A teeny, eeny, weeny, tee-ninetsy visitor!"

Yosip the Baker sat down at the table and held on to his red beard. As if he had taken a dose of magic medicine, he miraculously felt free of pain at that moment.

"A baby?" he whispered. He looked at Ginzl. Her smile reminded him of the Madonna.

"A baby, a baby!" gleefully sang Mordecai ben Yahbahbai. "Ginzl is with child! And guess who the godfather will be? Guess, guess, guess! No, do *not* guess, because I'm going to tell you! You, you, you, Yosip the Baker! The kindest man in God's universe, the embodiment of goodness, *you*! The godfather is *you*!"

The news dizzied Yosip the Baker, made his heart warm. Joyous tears began to roll down his cheeks and dampen his bandages and nestle in his beard like silver flowers in a red bush.

Laughing, sobbing, he said, "A baby. Oh, me. Oh, my. Me, a *godfather*."

To Ginzl, he promised, "I shall build a crib and put it by the window so the new baby can make friends with the clouds and wave back to the treetops."

To Liebeh, he lovingly said, "I shall teach you how to make tiny cakes for your little sister or brother to chew on. And when the baby is old enough, I shall sit nearby and watch and listen while you, Liebehle, teach it to sing and dance."

Finally, to Mordecai ben Yahbahbai, he said, "As for you, my dear friend, congratulations!" Gone and forgotten were last night's angry thoughts of taking Mordecai ben Yahbahbai by the back of the neck and throwing him all the way to Vitebsk. Gone for the moment were the burning and throbbing and stabbing pains from his beating.

The two men embraced each other until Mordecai ben Yahbahbai stepped back and said, "Thank you for the congratulations, my best friend. But one thing more. Now that I shall have *two* children, perhaps I should build a house of my own."

This surprised Yosip. Before he could reply, however, Mordecai ben Yahbahbai quickly added, "But suppose Shimkeh comes with our passports? What then?"

"The house would be wasted," said Yosip the Baker, trying not to laugh. "It is simple logic."

"Exactly! Logic!" agreed Mordecai ben Yahbahbai. "I would be in America—"

"And the house would be here."

"Ten thousand percent correct!"

"Therefore," chuckled Yosip the Baker, "logic says, 'Mordecai ben Yahbahbai, do not build a house.' Stay here, my friend. Do me the honor of living with me, at least until Shimkeh comes with the passports. Agreed?"

"Agreed," said Mordecai ben Yahbahbai. The two men shook hands. "And now, it is *your* turn."

"My turn?"

"Your turn. You said you had something to tell me."

"I said that?"

"I heard it, with these ears."

For the second time in his life and the second time in two days, Yosip the Baker lied. "Mordecai ben Yahbahbai, you heard wrong. I have nothing to talk to you about."

With that, Yosip turned away from Mordecai ben Yahbahbai and limped to the cupboard, preparing to go back to work.

"Yosip," urged Ginzl, "you must lie down and rest. Drink chicken soup. Until you are healed, I shall do the baking."

"Yes, yes," agreed Mordecai ben Yahbahbai. "Allow Ginzl to do the baking. Why must you work today? You're injured. Work tomorrow."

"No, no, my dear friends," said Yosip, fetching yeast, salt, rye seeds, and his huge wooden mixing bowl. "Thank you for your concern, but whether I am well or ill, happy or not so happy, I must bake every day, except for the Sabbath."

"Why? Where is it written?" asked Mordecai ben Yahbahbai.

"You know where it is written, Mordecai ben Yahbahbai. In the Good Book," replied Yosip, bending to take scoopfuls of flour from the barrel. "It says, 'No bread, no Bible.' If people have no bread, they will be too hungry and too angry to pay attention to the miracle of life. So baking is my duty. It is what I was put on this good earth to do." Measuring a cup of sugar and pouring it into his mixing bowl, he attempted to screw his battered face into a smile. "Also, I confess to the sin of vanity. People like to do what they do best, yes? I am a good baker, yes? Of course." He grinned at Mordecai ben Yahbahbai. "So, again, logic. Baking makes me feel good."

Sighing, but smiling, Ginzl returned to her cooking and Mordecai ben Yahbahbai took a book and sat in the sun near the window.

The rest of the day, Yosip kneaded and shaped the loaves of bread he would bake tomorrow morning. Every few minutes he looked up and watched Ginzl, filling the house with delicious cooking smells and the sounds of the song she sang. At other moments, he watched Mordecai ben Yahbahbai at the window, writing, reading, thinking, dozing, smiling in his sleep. But most of all, he watched little Liebeh, playing with her animal friends just outside the open door.

And Yosip the Baker put his fear of the Sergeant Major and his anger toward Mordecai ben Yahbahbai out of his mind and made peace with himself. For he knew his house was blessed with the sounds and vitality and beauty of happiness.

Yosip kneaded and shaped his loaves, Ginzl cooked and sang, Mordecai ben Yahbahbai dreamed, and Liebeh played.

7

SUMMER cooled into fall. Fall froze into winter. And when the new year arrived, so did the little visitor. They named him Dovidl.

Little Dovidl's face was handsome like Ginzl's, his arms and legs skinny like Mordecai ben Yahbahbai's, his voice strong and high-pitched like Liebeh's. Before he could even sit up by himself, the tiny visitor was given a lump of dough to play with. When he began to knead and roll and pat the lump of dough, everyone cried, "You see, Dovidl is like his godfather, Yosip the Baker!"

Blushing, Yosip the Baker put his hands beneath his round belly and pushed upward until his chest stuck out with pride and pleasure. From then on, each time the little visitor's dimpled hands touched the lump of dough, Yosip the Baker felt Dovidl's tiny fingers within him, kneading and patting and capturing his heart.

One season sped into another. Spring came. Melting snow muddied the road. Sleeping fields wakened. Animals in the forest stirred. Summer approached. Buds flowered. Hatchlings tested their wings, flying in larger and larger circles around their nests until one day they flew away, never to return. Dovidl began to crawl. He knew every inch of the floor in Yosip's house. Liebeh and Yuri played tag, made castles of sand, walked along the road, waded in the brook. She chattered to him about her memories of the city. He introduced her to the mysteries of the forest. Every morning, Yosip the Baker and Ginzl baked. Every night, Mordecai ben Yahbahbai told his stories to Yuri and his parents and sisters and Uncle Oleg and all the other woodchoppers and their families.

And, day after day, week after week, month after month, Shimkeh did not come with the passports.

ON a hot and dusty summer day, Liebeh and Yuri sat on a shaded mossy rock beneath the gnarled oak tree near Yosip the Baker's house and silently watched their tiny animal friends busy themselves, bees buzzing, butterflies fluttering, jays swooping and darting and scolding, woodchucks clambering and chattering.

But suddenly, as if all the woodland creatures sensed danger in a language unknown to humans, every animal paused, froze, then disappeared.

Perplexed, Liebeh and Yuri looked at each other for a moment. After a few seconds, however, they realized very well what alarmed the animals. Softly at first, then more and more ominously,?there reverberated a distant rumbling and clanking.

"It's the third day of the seventh month," Yuri muttered. And just as he had done the previous summer, he jumped to his feet and hurried home to protect his mother and sisters.

And again, breathlessly, Liebeh ran into Yosip's house, shouting, "Cossacks! Cossacks are coming!"

And once more, Mordecai ben Yahbahbai began to weep, partly from fear, partly from rage. "How can I be in the Czar's army and in America at the same time?" Looking skyward, he angrily blubbered, "Does *anybody* know the answer? What happened to logic?"

Just as he did the previous summer, Yosip the Baker hid Mordecai ben Yahbahbai. But this time it was decided they would conceal him beneath Yosip the Baker's great fluffy feather mattress. As Mordecai ben Yahbahbai, his black beard wet from crying, spread his arms wide and begged heaven for guidance, once more Yosip grabbed him by the back of the neck and the seat of the pants and, with a mighty heave upward, lifted the tearful little man onto the cot and stuffed him under the bedding.

Once more, although sobbing, Mordecai ben Yahbahbai had a question to ask. His head popped out from beneath the mattress and he wailed, "Yosip? Yosip, my friend?"

"What is it? You must be quiet or the cossacks will hear you," Yosip the Baker whispered.

"There's something here, under the mattress, such as, perhaps, maybe—a flask? Yes. A flask—a flask of water. No. Not water. A flask of vodka!" wept Mordecai ben Yahbahbai.

"Don't worry about it. Leave it alone. It doesn't bite," answered Yosip.

"What if I take a drink?" asked Mordecai ben Yahbahbai.

"Be my guest. Take two drinks."

"But vodka makes me sing. What if I begin to sing?"

"Then you'll spend the next five years of your life singing in the glorious army of the Czar, and, believe me, there you won't be singing a happy song."

"You're right, Yosip. So here's what I'll do—I'll take a drink—no, I'll take *two* drinks, as you suggested—but I won't sing." And Mordecai ben Yahbahbai's head disappeared under Yosip's fluffy mattress.

Once more, Liebeh hid, this time in one of the empty canvas bags in which Yosip sent bread to Vitebsk and Smolensk. Once more, the keg of sugar served as a hiding place, this time for the new baby, Dovidl.

"What if the baby makes a wee-wee in the sugar?" Liebeh asked.

"Then Dovidl will have invented a new kind of candy," answered Ginzl, who again crawled, headfirst, into the bottom of the cupboard and again got stuck in the doorway. This time, however, Yosip the Baker had to give her two mighty pushes from behind before she became unstuck and tumbled inside.

Shutting and bolting the cupboard door, Yosip the Baker again said a prayer and, once more, went outside to face the soldiers. Once more, the Sergeant Major read from the parchment (even though he knew it by heart). Once more, Yosip the Baker said there was no one here but himself. Once more, the cossacks demanded he bake them a meal. Once more, Yosip the Baker said he had no food.

Once more, the Sergeant Major beat and kicked Yosip the Baker without mercy. And, once more, as the soldiers rode away leaving him lying in the dust, bloody and bruised, Yosip the Baker was aware of only one thing.

Just in front of his eyes, gleaming in the dirt beside his battered face, lay another of his strong, white teeth.

Although it hurt him to move, he felt inside his mouth with his finger and counted his teeth. One. Two. Three. Four. Five. Six. Seven. Eight.

Eight teeth left.

Groaning, Yosip the Baker struggled to his feet and stumbled into the house; unbolted the cupboard door and released Ginzl; pulled Mordecai ben Yahbahbai, who smelled from vodka and was having a hard time not singing, from beneath the mattress; opened the canvas bag and freed Liebeh; removed the top from the sugar keg and gave Ginzl her tiny Dovidl, who had not invented a new kind of candy; and sighed through his bloody, cut lips, "We are safe now. The soldiers have gone."

THAT night, as he tried to sleep, Yosip the Baker once more decided to order Mordecai ben Yahbahbai to go to Vitebsk, find Shimkeh, and bring back the passports.

So the next morning, once more, he said to Mordecai ben Yahbahbai, "I must talk to you."

And, once more, Mordecai ben Yahbahbai answered, "First, me. I must talk to *you*. I am exploding with news."

"Very well," sighed Yosip the Baker. "You first. What is your news?"

"Simply this." Mordecai ben Yahbahbai beamed. "You, Yosip the Baker, are going to have a *visitor*!"

"I already have *four* visitors," Yosip answered.

"And now, you are going to have *another* one! A teeny, weeny, ee-ninetsy visitor!"

"Another baby, yes?" whispered Yosip the Baker.

"Yes, yes! And guess who will be the new visitor's godfather? *You*, Yosip the Baker! The kindest man in God's universe, the embodiment of goodness, *you* will be the godfather!"

Once more, tears rolled down Yosip the Baker's cheeks and nestled in his beard like crystal flowers in a red bush. Once more, he decided not to grab Mordecai ben Yahbahbai by the back of the neck and throw him all the way to Vitebsk, even though, at that moment, he wanted desperately to do it. Once more, he refused to think about his newly missing tooth and how badly the Sergeant Major had hurt him.

Instead, he thought of how blessed was his house, to be so full of warmth and happiness. Instead, he began fashioning another crib to put near the window so the new visitor could look out and see how the sky moved and the saucy robins played on the windowsill.

And a few weeks later, when Ginzl said, "Beloved Yosip, your wounds are more than we can bear, and my husband and I have decided to go back to Vitebsk so next year when the cossacks come there will be no one to hide and you can invite the soldiers into your house and the Sergeant Major will not beat you," Yosip the Baker told her she was like his daughter and her children were his godchildren and the place where nobody stopped would be cold and empty without them and all the beatings in the world were worth the happiness her family gave him, and he implored them to stay.

And a few weeks after that, when Mordecai ben Yahbahbai said, "Yosip, my dearest and everlasting friend, my conscience torments me and I've decided to enlist in the army so never again will you be beaten on my account, and Ginzl and the children will go to Vitebsk and wait for me while I'm a soldier," Yosip argued that it would be a tragedy and a sin if he, Mordecai ben Yahbahbai, unnecessarily deserted his loved ones for five years and missed seeing his children grow up, and Yosip convinced Mordecai ben Yahbahbai that it would be wrong for him to volunteer to serve in the glorious army of the Czar.

And a few weeks after that, when Mordecai ben Yahbahbai said, "Since we are not leaving and are soon to have our third child, I *must* build a house of my own," Yosip the Baker reminded him that if Shimkeh came with the passports, the new house would be wasted, so it was only logical for Mordecai ben Yahbahbai, Ginzl, Liebeh, Dovidl, and the expected new visitor to remain here, in this house, with him.

Five months later the new year came. So did the new visitor. This new visitor—they named her Fraydl—had a dimpled, heart-shaped face and plump, shapely arms and legs, but she was just like the first new visitor when it came to the heart of Yosip the Baker.

He was her prisoner from the first moment she reached out her tiny hands and held on to his red beard with the unbreakable grip of a baby's love.

8

WINTER, spring, summer, and on the third day of the seventh month, the cossacks again swept down on the place where nobody stopped.

Yosip the Baker lost another tooth.

Mordecai ben Yahbahbai announced that another new visitor was coming.

Sure enough, when January came the third new visitor arrived on schedule. Meanwhile, Shimkeh did not arrive with the passports.

And, again, everything began to happen in the same way in the place where nobody stopped.

In the fourth year, another tooth went, another visitor came, and not a trace of Shimkeh with the passports.

In the fifth year, another tooth lost, another visitor found. And no Shimkeh.

Six years, six teeth, six visitors, no Shimkeh.

ALL this time, Yosip the Baker kept a secret, a small and delicious secret he shared with no one—not even with Ginzl, whom he loved as if he were her father—not even with his adored Liebeh, whom he loved as if he were her grandfather.

What was the secret Yosip the Baker shared with no one? It had to do with a tiny blue velvet bag lined in red silk.

From his childhood years, he dimly remembered that his mother had kept a pearl necklace in it. The necklace had disappeared when his mother died. He had been less then ten years of age then. But somehow young Yosip got possession of that empty small velvet bag. It was the only thing he had left to remind him of his mother. Throughout his manhood, even when he was in the army, he carried it with him at all times in his shirt pocket next to his heart.

But merely having the velvet bag was not Yosip the Baker's secret. So what *was* the secret? The secret was what he now had in the bag.

Every time he was beaten and humiliated by the Sergeant Major and lost another tooth, Yosip found the tooth in the dirt, carefully washed and rubbed it dry, and put it in the bag.

After six years, there were six teeth in the bag. And, of course, each tooth had a name. Dovidl was tooth number one, Fraydl tooth number two, Deeneh number

---

Yosip the Baker poured the teeth into the palm of his hand, one for each of his six new visitors.

three, Ya'akov number four, Moishl number five, and, now, Ahvrom Tevyeh number six.

And whenever Yosip the Baker felt that he could take no more beatings and tell no more lies, every time his heart felt like a heavy, burning rock inside his chest, every time his nightmares woke him from his cot in a panic, every time his dear friend Mordecai ben Yahbahbai the scholar did something so foolish that Yosip the Baker had to go outside and throw stones through the air instead of staying inside and throwing Mordecai ben Yahbahbai through the window—every time Yosip the Baker felt sad or angry or hurt—he went off by himself, took the blue velvet bag from the shirt pocket next to his heart, poured the teeth into the palm of his hand, and said, "Dovidl, Fraydl, Deeneh, Ya'akov, Moishl, Ahvrom Tevyeh," over and over again, until his melancholy vanished and his happiness returned.

LITTLE Dovidl was now five years old. Sometimes he was like his father, making up poems and stories and talking and talking and talking. He chatted with trees, conversed with bees, had one-sided discussions with the sky or with chickens or one of his infant brothers or sisters—he talked to anyone who would listen.

Other times Dovidl was like his sister Liebeh, musical and beautiful and a bit mischievous. And strange as it may seem, Dovidl's idol was tall and athletic Yuri, now sixteen, who taught him to swing an ax, clean fish with a hunting knife, protect himself with his fists, and catch rats and mice.

From his mama Dovidl received his strength of character and a loving heart. But most of the time, Dovidl was like his godfather, Yosip the Baker, calm, wise, hardworking, and devoted.

Year in, year out, Mordecai ben Yahbahbai watched his eldest son closely and was pleased with what he saw. Finally, one afternoon he called Dovidl to him and said, "My dear boy, since you are no longer a baby, today you embark upon a new journey into the most glorious dimension a human being can explore. Today I shall begin to teach you how to read and write—and how to use your mind."

From then on, every afternoon, while Yosip the Baker sifted, measured, and mixed, and Ginzl cooked, and Liebeh, now twelve years old, cared for the babies, Dovidl and his father sat together at the table, books open, and pencils, pieces of paper, and chalk and slate nearby.

The small boy was an eager and quick and obedient pupil. In just a few weeks he was reciting the alphabet and drawing letters and words.

But one day, as father and son began their lesson, Liebeh sat down next to them and said, "Papa, may I also have a book and a pencil and paper? Teach me also to read and write, Papa. Please."

After a surprised moment, Mordecai ben Yahbahbai said, gently but firmly, "Liebehle, my darling child, you are a girl. In this world of ours, which I did not create, girls help their mamas. Boys study books."

"But I can do both," she insisted. "I'm different, Papa. Please, teach me how to read and write."

"You are not different, Liebeh. Don't be so stubborn. You are a girl. Dovidl is a boy." Impatiently, he added, "And I am your father, who tells you what to do, and you are my daughter who obeys me."

"Yuri says I can do anything a boy can do. He taught me to track and climb and swim. He says my brain is better than a boy's. He says I know things no boy in this place will ever know."

"Yuri?" laughed Mordecai ben Yahbahbai. "Yuri says this and Yuri says that. You quote him like he's King Solomon or William Shakespeare. Who is Yuri? He's an ignorant serf, pretty to look at, I'm sure. Where is Yuri? In the dark forest, cutting down trees at the age of sixteen. Liebehle, when he is a hundred and sixteen, may he live that long in good health, your philosopher Yuri will still be cutting down trees."

Blinking back tears, Liebeh set her beautiful jaw and refused to budge from the table. "Papa, please say yes. Please."

"Enough! How can I say yes when I already said no? No. And no again. That is my decision."

Liebeh's face darkened into a stubborn frown. "And here is *my* decision," she answered, sharply. "I will *so* learn to read and write."

"You argue with your father? You open a mouth to me? The fourth commandment, Liebeh. Honor thy father and mother. Shame on you. Now be silent. Go away from the table. Help Mama with the babies. Dovidl and I have work to do."

The old saying is, Like father, like son. In the case of Mordecai ben Yahbahbai and Liebeh it was like father, like daughter—a strong-willed man and his equally strong-willed child.

For a few seconds, their eyes locked in anger and hurt and love and determination. Finally, her back stiff, teeth clenched, determined not to cry, more resolved than ever, Liebeh rose from the table and exclaimed, "I will so! I will so! You'll see!" and ran from the room.

"You will apologize for talking to your father like that!" Mordecai ben Yahbahbai called after her, but she was already gone.

For a long and silent moment Mordecai ben Yahbahbai looked out the window, avoiding the eyes of Ginzl and Yosip, and debated within his mind whether he had done right or wrong.

First he lifted one hand, palm upward, then the other hand the same way, all the while nodding his head up and down or to and fro, sometimes shrugging his shoulders, as if two different people were inside him having an argument. He opened his arms wide in frustration, looked toward heaven for guidance, and finding none, turned to Dovidl and shouted, "So why are you sitting there doing nothing, like a glump on a cabbage? Are you here to act like a simpleton or are you here to learn? Take your pencil in your hand and write for me the alphabet, all the way through, and may God help you if you make a mistake."

FOR many weeks, each sorrowing in his and her own way, Liebeh and her father, both as headstrong as mules, avoided each other like two strangers. And then, suddenly, as if their disagreement had never occurred, Liebeh became herself again, an enchanting child, and Mordecai ben Yahbahbai once more was able to show his daughter how much he loved her.

Months passed. Dovidl began to learn so rapidly that his father allowed him to go to the leather valises and wooden trunks and select grown-up books to read. Constantly smiling and agreeing with himself that he was a most extraordinary teacher, Mordecai ben Yahbahbai took great pride in his son's progress.

These were golden days in the home of Yosip the Baker. Everyone in the household got along well with everyone else. Liebeh, especially, was a joy to her father, loving and sweet and radiant. And every day after lunch, during Dovidl's lessons, she obediently disappeared from sight.

One afternoon, however, as father and son were having their lesson, Mordecai ben Yahbahbai decided he wanted a glass of tea.

"Ginzl," he called. "Tea."

No answer came from Ginzl.

Peering out through the window, Mordecai ben Yahbahbai saw, far away from the house at the edge of the woods, Ginzl and Yosip the Baker, along with Fraydl, Deeneh, Ya'akov, Moishl, and even the baby, Ahvrom Tevyeh, picking berries from which Yosip would make syrup for his raisin-filled babkas.

"I need a glass of tea," complained Mordecai ben Yahbahbai. "Liebeh! Liebeh, where are you?" he called. "Your father wants tea."

But all he heard in response was silence.

"So, Dovidl, this once, will it kill your papa to make a glass of tea himself? Never mind, don't tell me. Read your book. Later, I will ask you about what you are reading. And God help you if you do not give me the right answers."

Usually, Dovidl smiled inwardly when his father made such threats. Mordecai ben Yahbahbai was a gentle man. But this afternoon, Dovidl's face tightened with apprehension as he watched his father go to the cupboard and look for the can of tea leaves. "Where does she keep it? All I see is everything but tea," muttered Mordecai ben Yahbahbai. He looked around the room, and brightened. "Aha, I know where it is. In the closet."

In one corner of the room, partitioned off by a cloth hung on a rope, was a small, triangular closet.

"I'll make tea for you, Papa," said Dovidl, his voice anxious.

"I told you, read the book. Logic, Dovidl, logic. How can you make tea and read the book at the same time?"

As Dovidl's frightened eyes followed him, Mordecai ben Yahbahbai crossed the room, went to the small pantry, pulled the cloth partition aside—and gasped as he looked into the closet. There, sitting cross-legged on the floor, books beside her, a pencil in her hand, a tablet in her lap, sat Liebeh.

Fear and surprise froze her lovely face as she looked up at her father. Shocked, he furrowed his brow. His jaw and chin turned to rock. For a moment, neither moved, or even breathed.

"You sit here every day, on the floor in this closet, and listen while I teach Dovidl?" he asked.

She nodded.

He studied his daughter as if he had never really looked at her before.

"And may I see?" asked Mordecai ben Yahbahbai, holding out his hand, requesting her tablet. When she

gave it to him, he studied the tablet, turning the pages, looking hard at each one.

"And a book, please? That one." She handed him the book he asked for. His eyebrows lifted with surprise when he saw the name of the book. "You took these books from my valise?"

She nodded solemnly.

Turning to his son, Mordecai ben Yahbahbai stared at the boy for a moment before he asked, "And you, Dovidl? Did you know Liebeh was here every day, sitting in the closet during our lesson?"

Dovidl looked squarely into his father's eyes and whispered, respectfully, "Yes, Papa."

"Aha. And you helped her get the books from my valise?"

Again, Dovidl's gaze did not waver. "Yes, Papa," the boy replied, softly.

"And you showed her each day what I had taught you?"

"Yes, Papa."

Something was happening inside Mordecai ben Yahbahbai. His face and manner were still cold, but inside his heart was about to melt. It was difficult for him to keep from smiling.

Again he turned to Liebeh. Opening the book, he turned to a certain page and handed it back to her.

"Read," he commanded.

And even though she stumbled over a word here and there, Liebeh, in a voice as true as music, read, "If you

---

There, cross-legged on the floor, books beside her and a tablet in her lap, sat Liebeh.

had your eyes, you might fail of the knowing me: it is a wise father that knows his own child."

"Enough," said Mordecai ben Yahbahbai. His face, so icy a moment before, warmed as if the sun suddenly shone through the clouds on a gloomy winter day.

"Sometimes I am not such a wise father. Forgive me, my indescribably beautiful daughter, for not knowing who you are."

He held out his hand to her, helped her to her feet, and said, laughing, "Do you know of whom you remind me? Of myself. Yes, me—when I was your age. I also had a hunger to discover new worlds. I also questioned the ways of my father." He laughed again and glanced slyly at Dovidl. "I did not, however, have a helper." Putting his arm around Liebeh's shoulder and hugging her, he said, "My Liebehle, we have our differences, but there is one thing on which I am certain we agree—it is much more comfortable to sit on a chair at the table than on the floor in a dark closet. Come, my child. You sit on my right, and your little brother—your co-conspirator, Master Dovidl—will sit on my left."

"Thank you, Papa," she whispered, throwing her arms around him. "There is so much I want to learn from you."

"Yes, Liebehle. And I shall learn from you."

9

BY the time Liebeh was sixteen, she had read all the books in her father's worn leather valises and wooden trunks. As she began to reread them she understood more each time through and marveled at the revelations and ideas not apparent to her at first.

Sometimes sudden meaning flashed into her consciousness like a lamp lit in a black cavern and for an exquisite and unforgettable instance everything became clear and beautiful. On those occasions she laughed out loud, and Ginzl, momentarily startled, would look at her daughter, then smile at the picture of her lovely eldest child, sitting cross-legged on the floor in a corner, absorbed in a book. Other times the leather-covered, worn volumes left Liebeh in bittersweet pain or rage or despair. Certain pages bore small circlets where her tears had dropped on the yellowed paper and dried—she wept because of the slings and arrows of weak and tormented Hamlet's outrageous fortune, Juliet's pure and tragic love, Iago's treachery, Shylock's vengeful fury.

Mordecai ben Yahbahbai treated his daughter as most adoring fathers always behave toward their firstborn girls.

He babied her and refused to acknowledge the fact that she was now a young woman. But in one particular way he acted toward her as if she were his peer. She and he spent the better part of many afternoons talking about what was in the books, debating, analyzing, agreeing, disagreeing, like two Talmudic scholars trying to understand the words of their God. He still had much to teach her, but her quick mind and progress made him even more loving, if that were possible.

DOVIDL, on the other hand, seven years younger than Liebeh, still lived in the world of a nine-year-old boy. Yes, he had a brain as agile as his older sister's; he undoubtedly possessed great sensitivity and had the soul of an artist. No one could question his ability to sing and write poetry and understand ideas. He was a loving and lovable boy and worked as hard as an adult, helping Yosip and his mother with the baking, doing most of the chores around the house, and assisting his father in teaching his little brothers and sisters the alphabet.

But Dovidl also liked to be outdoors with the other young boys who lived in the place where nobody stopped and run and jump and yell like a wild man and wrestle and have snowball wars and explore caves in the cliff below the waterfall and scale the tallest pine in the forest and build a tree house and sit in it and look out over the forest's carpet of treetops to the meadows and orchards and winding road and snaking river until all disappeared where the horizon met the sky. He and his friends liked to crouch down unseen near the road and watch travelers hurry by on horseback or in their wagons or coaches and speculate as to who these strangers were and where they were going. He liked to sit astride an old cow, imagining it a war-horse, and joust with a wooden sword he had whittled himself with Yuri's big hunting knife.

Yuri was Dovidl's hero. Just as Yuri had taught Liebeh about the beauties and mysteries of the forest, so did he instruct her eager little brother on how to protect himself in a fight, how to use the many tools in Yosip's shed, harness an ox, milk a goat, hurdle a tree stump while running at full speed, swim in the icy creek. He taught Dovidl how to dance peasant dances and sing rustic songs Mordecai ben Yahbahbai had never heard.

Now a strapping man of almost twenty, over six feet in height, his muscles made hard as obsidian from chopping wood from dawn to dusk since he was fifteen, Yuri became like an older brother to Dovidl. Each night, when everyone gathered to listen to Mordecai ben Yahbahbai's stories and sing and dance, Dovidl sat between Liebeh and Yuri, the two young people he loved more than any others. And although he was as rapt as anyone by his father's stories, Dovidl studied the faces of Liebeh and Yuri for their reactions to all they heard. When everyone swayed to a song or tapped their feet to a dance tempo, Dovidl watched Yuri and Liebeh and tried to do as they did.

On the Sabbath, when Yuri came to the door in his best clothes, Dovidl often accompanied his big sister and the young woodchopper on their Sunday afternoon strolls. And so preoccupied was Dovidl with being with Yuri, walking like Yuri, singing like Yuri, smiling like Yuri, that never once did he realize that Liebeh, although a loving and rare sister, did not always want her little brother around. She, too, liked Yuri, and sometimes wanted to be alone with him.

TEN years is not a long time to a mountain or an ocean. If you think about it, ten *thousand* years is not a long time to a mountain or an ocean.

But many things can happen to human beings in ten years, even in the place where nobody stopped, where everything always happened the same way.

So it came to pass that during the decade since Mordecai ben Yahbahbai, Ginzl, and Liebeh first came to live in the house of Yosip the Baker, ten new visitors came to stay, ten little brothers and sisters for Liebeh to look after, which meant that Yosip the Baker became a godfather ten times.

And, of course, each year on the third day of the seventh month the Sergeant Major knocked out one of his teeth, so that now the aging baker had ten teeth in his secret velvet bag and none in his mouth.

In the meantime, Yosip the Baker's small stone house had grown a bit. First he built a small bedroom for Mordecai ben Yahbahbai and Ginzl, then another bedroom for the boy children, followed by another for the girl children, and, finally, a tiny bedroom for Liebeh as a present on her sixteenth birthday. But even though they all had their own quarters, in the arctic winter everyone still slept in the big main room near the lifesaving warmth of the great stone oven.

Noah's Ark probably was less crowded than the house of Yosip the Baker. Wherever you walked, you bumped into a crib or almost stepped on a baby or stumbled on a book or nearly tripped over a bag of freshly baked bread. Also, sometimes it was very noisy, particularly in the afternoons, when Liebeh and Dovidl helped their father teach their younger brothers and sisters to read, and each child recited aloud at the same time from a different book. During those afternoon lessons, instead of Noah's Ark, Yosip's house was more like the Tower of Babel.

In the evenings life in the cottage became even busier and more crowded. When the neighbors congregated and Mordecai ben Yahbahbai sat before them on a high stool, all he could see was faces, each listener so close to the next that not a bare inch of floor or table or bench could be seen. And the philosophers who once argued about how many angels could dance on the head of a pin should have seen how many of Ginzl's small children, while their papa told stories, could sit on their godfather—Simchl on Yosip the Baker's right knee, Ahvrom Tevyeh and little Timmeh Layeh on his left knee, tiny Boruch on his shoulder, the infant Rochl in his arms, Deeneh in his lap, Fraydl on the floor between his legs, Ya'akov on his right foot, and Moishl on his left foot—like a host of cherubs resting on a fluffy cloud.

Liebeh always sat next to the old man, and she and Dovidl, perched between his older sister and Yuri, showed their love for Yosip by often reaching out and touching his arm.

So even though he had no teeth left and ate only porridge and soft bread soaked in milk, and even though his once-red beard had whitened so that its few remaining red hairs stood out like trickles of blood on a snow-covered bush—never during those ten years, never for a minute, or a day, a week, a month, a year—never ever—did Yosip the Baker forget what a terrible curse loneliness had been and what a rare blessing happiness is.

And each night in bed, before he softly descended into the peaceful nonbeing of sleep, he prayed that Shimkeh would never come with the passports.

10

SHIMKEH hid behind a wall of hedges near the Vitebsk stagecoach depot and peered through bushes wet with early morning dew. Even though he was a short man, not much taller than a child, and had heavy bones inside a thick body, he didn't look fat. Instead, he resembled a cheery, energetic gnome. Vitality radiated from him like sparks from burning green wood.

Behind him, also hidden by the hedge, stood his wife Froomeh, so tall and stately that even when Shimkeh stood up straight the top of his head was well below her exquisite face. She made no attempt to hide herself, but merely watched Shimkeh.

In an effort to get a better view of the coach being hitched to a team of horses, he bent, he craned his neck, he moved his head this way, that way, up, down, while his nervous feet did a little dance in place. His jet black eyes seemed like two tiny holes in his head, and he seldom blinked, as if he didn't in his lifetime ever want to miss one fraction of a second of what he was seeing.

"Froomeh, my beautiful love," hissed Shimkeh, "do you have the letter?"

"Which letter?" queried Froomeh. Her elegant brow wrinkled just a bit, as if it hurt her to think.

Shimkeh turned and stared up at his wife.

"My angelic goddess," he said, his voice full of loving kindness, "how many letters have I ever given you to hold for me?"

She thought for a moment and then replied, "One?"

He beamed. "Yes! One. My Venus, where is it? My Helen of Troy, where is the letter?"

"I know where," she answered proudly. Opening her handbag and taking out a sealed white envelope, she chirped, "Here it is!"

"Excellent!" gushed Shimkeh, as if addressing a small child. "Now listen closely. Are you listening?"

"I think so."

"Exemplary!" As he spoke to her, he said each word slowly and clearly. "Stroll over to the stagecoach driver and give him the letter and say to him, 'This letter is for Mordecai ben Yahbahbai, who lives in the place where nobody stops,' and then give him these five kopeks." He looked at her intently, as if trying to determine whether or not her brain was working. "Do you understand?"

"Give the driver the letter and five kopeks."

"Mag-*ni*-fi-cent! And say to him—what?"

"Say to him, um, say to him . . ." Her lips pursed as she struggled to remember. After a moment, however, she brightened. Although her smile was as stunning as her face, it was also as empty. "Say to him, 'The five kopeks are for Mordecai ben Yahbahbai in the place where nobody stops.' "

"Almost!" encouraged Shimkeh. "The five kopeks are for the *driver*. The *letter* is for my cousin, Mordecai ben Yahbahbai."

"Yes," she said to herself, repeating the words. "Five kopeks. Driver. Letter. Cousin Mordecai ben Yahbahbai."

"I love you. You are the stupidest woman in the world—and the most ravishingly beautiful."

"Thank you," she answered sincerely.

"I apologize for taxing you in this way, but if I show myself and give the driver the letter, someone who knows me might see me and tell the police. Then you would be all alone for ten or maybe twenty years. Who would look after you? Not I. I'd be in a salt mine in Siberia."

He stood on his tiptoes and kissed her chin. "Any questions?" he asked her.

After a pause, she replied, "Yes."

"Ask, my Aphrodite. Ask. What is your question?"

After another pause, as if to gather the right words, she asked, "Which one is the driver?"

Sighing, Shimkeh said, "My ideal, my embodiment of adorableness, do you see that man sitting alone on top of the stagecoach with the reins in his hands?"

"Yes."

"*He* is the driver."

As if she had just discovered the secret to all truths in the universe, her huge, incredibly stunning eyes became even brighter, and she said, "Oh!"

"Now go, my nymph, my eternal love. Go!"

Apprehensively, he watched as she walked around the hedge and into the clear. Beads of nervous perspiration suddenly covered his flat, intelligent face. He crouched. He clenched and unclenched his fists. He prayed to himself.

Froomeh walked toward the stagecoach, but as she crossed the depot yard and approached the driver, sitting high atop the vehicle, Shimkeh relaxed and began to grin. Every head in sight had turned for a glimpse of his graceful, regal, beautiful wife, who attracted admiration as surely as would a great work of art. In her presence, no one noticed him, as if he were invisible—a desirable asset for a man like Shimkeh.

Froomeh spoke to the driver, who took his cap off and stared at her incomparable face. Had she asked him to drive over the side of a cliff, he probably would have done so willingly. Instead, after a moment he reached down and, nodding his head, took the letter and coins from Froomeh.

Shimkeh did a little jig of satisfaction. He gleefully rubbed his stubby hands together, as his face widened into an even greater and more satisfied grin.

DOVIDL worked harder in the middle of the morning than any other time of day. It was then that his mother and Yosip the Baker began the demanding task of mixing and measuring the ingredients that would be tomorrow's baked goods, and it therefore became Dovidl's responsibility to look after everything else.

This morning he repaired a section of the fence in front of the cottage. Last night a cow had pushed against it and knocked it flat. Before the chickens could be let out of the coop to forage in the yard for worms and feed, the fallen pickets had to be fixed.

As he hammered a post into the soft earth, he heard the stagecoach approaching, as it did each day at this time—if the weather allowed. Sometimes snow or mud delayed it and the bread-filled bags were not picked up from the sheltered roadside stone table until afternoon.

As the carriage slowed and stopped, Dovidl paused long enough to watch the driver jump down from his high seat as he always did and gather the bags and lash them to the rear of the coach. The boy never tired of seeing the team of lathered and wild-eyed horses, nor of speculating who rode inside the coach and what it would be like to be such a passenger traveling to exotic, foreign places.

Today, however, instead of climbing back up to his seat and proceeding on his way, the driver waved to Dovidl and beckoned to him. Surprised, the youngster put his mallet down and walked quickly to the road.

"Boy," said the driver, "do you know someone in this place named, um—" He took an envelope from inside his shirt and read, "Um, Mordecai ben Yahbahboo."

"Yahbahbai," Dovidl replied. "He's my father."

"This is for him." The driver gave Dovidl the envelope.

"Thank you, sir," said Dovidl.

"You're welcome," the driver called over his shoulder as he climbed back on the coach. From his high seat he cried to the horses, "Eeeeyah! Gittup!" His whip cracked. The team strained forward in their traces. The coach began moving away, slowly at first and then faster and faster.

For a moment Dovidl idly examined the envelope, but suddenly his eyebrows shot up and he exclaimed, "Oooh! Could it be from Shimkeh? What if the passports are inside?"

Running to the house, he shouted, "Papa! Papa! A

letter for you! Maybe from Shimkeh! Maybe it's the passports!"

Bursting through the door, he stopped just inside the cottage. They had heard his shouts. Like frozen statues, everyone stared at him—Mordecai ben Yahbahbai from his chair by the window, Yosip and Ginzl at the flour-covered table, Liebeh in the middle of the big room holding Rochl, the youngest visitor, in her arms, and all the rest of Dovidl's little brothers and sisters. For a few seconds no one moved.

Dovidl interrupted the hush in the room. Holding the envelope out toward his father, he whispered, "A letter for you, Papa."

Mordecai ben Yahbahbai rose slowly from his chair, took the letter, and examined it.

"Oh, Papa, open it!" Liebeh cried.

"Yes. Open it," said Ginzl.

"I'm in no hurry," replied Mordecai ben Yahbahbai. "It's not every day that a dream comes true. I wish to savor this moment."

"Before you decide whether it's a dream or a nightmare, I suggest you open it, Mordecai," advised Ginzl.

Smiling, he responded, "Believe me, my Ginzl, it's a dream."

"Open it, my friend," said Yosip the Baker. Unlike Mordecai ben Yahbahbai, he was not smiling. His ancient heart pounded at the dreadful prospect of an envelope full of passports. "Open it," he repeated softly to himself.

"I'll tell you what I'll do. I'll open it," laughed Mordecai ben Yahbahbai, and with a flourish he ripped open the envelope.

But the envelope contained only a single sheet of paper.

His spirits dampened, Mordecai ben Yahbahbai looked into the envelope, held it upside down and shook it, and looked again, but there were no passports—only the one lonely single piece of paper, densely covered with handwriting.

Glancing at the bottom of the letter's page, however, he began to smile. "Aha," he said triumphantly. "It's from—guess who? Shimkeh!"

Everyone in the room cheered—except for Yosip, who looked on solemnly, and Ginzl, who stared at the letter.

"Read it, Mordecai," she again said.

"I'll tell you what I'll do. I'll read it," he replied in a jubilant voice. "It may take a few minutes. The writing is very small and there is a great deal of it."

Again the room became very quiet. The children all watched their father in happy anticipation as he held the letter to the window's light to get a better view and began reading it to himself.

But as he read, Mordecai ben Yahbahbai's cheery countenance became sadder and sadder. By the time he reached the bottom of the page, the lines in his face had deepened into gloom.

"Mordecai?" whispered Ginzl tenderly.

"You were correct, my wife. It's a nightmare." He could hardly speak. Staring past them into his own misery, he crumpled the letter and stuffed it into his pocket.

"What does the letter say, Papa?" asked Liebeh.

"Later, Liebehle," said Ginzl. To Mordecai ben Yahbahbai she said, "Come with me, my sweetheart." She took his hand and began leading him toward the door. To Liebeh she said, "Feed the children, Liebehle." To her eldest son she said, "Help Yosip, Dovidl." To Yosip she said, "My husband and I are going out for a walk."

"Yes—go," said Yosip the Baker. "We'll be fine." Trying to conceal his anxiety, the old man picked up a pitcher and began filling a measuring cup with milk.

GINZL and Mordecai ben Yahbahbai sat on a large boulder on the bank of a brook not too far from Yosip the Baker's house. They came here sometimes to talk. Usually Mordecai ben Yahbahbai did most of that, but today his silence left Ginzl perturbed.

"Read me the letter, my love," she finally said.

"I am too ashamed," he answered. Sick at heart, he added, "You are right, my precious wife, and I am wrong. My cousin Shimkeh is a liar and a thief."

"Read me the letter, Mordecai," she repeated.

"Very well," he sighed. He took the wadded-up sheet of paper from his pocket, straightened it, and read:

> "My Esteemed Cousin,
>
> "Are you still in the place where I told you to wait? I hope so, because I would like to come and visit you for a little while. I just finished a business transaction and I need to go somewhere and rest, a place where I am not known, a place where I won't be bothered while I think about my next venture. So I thought of you.

"Read me the letter, my love," Ginzl said to Mordecai ben Yahbahbai.

"I am now married to a very beautiful woman who would come with me. Her name is Froomeh bas Itzig. She is as lovely as your Ginzl, if that is possible.

"I am still working on acquiring your passports. Even if you have more children by now, don't worry. Children are allowed to travel under their parents' papers. I know you've waited a long time, but my friend who works for the Czar's Bureau of Passports, to whom I paid your ninety rubles, now tells me it won't be much longer. When dealing with bureaucrats, we must be patient, ha, ha. So as I said, don't worry. Some people wait much longer than ten years before they are able to go to America. Getting passports isn't easy. I haven't even been able to get one for myself. Otherwise, I'd go with you. I think I could do very well in America. Anyway, as I said twice already, don't worry. In our youth you were always full of faith. I hope you are still full of it.

"Please write me a letter, but don't address it to me. *Don't use my name*. I don't want certain businessmen to know where I am. Send your reply to Froomeh bas Itzig, General Post Office, Vitebsk. Give it to the stagecoach driver. Tell him to bring it to Vitebsk and post it there. And as I said three times already, don't worry.

"Your Loving and Respectful First Cousin,

"Shimkeh ben Yussel"

By the time he finished reading the letter, Mordecai ben Yahbahbai's tears had dampened his black beard. Instead of a vigorous man of forty-five, he looked like a defeated and frightened ninety-year-old. His red-rimmed eyes now seemed as small and fierce as a rooster's. His skin had drawn tightly over his thin facial bones. He sat hunched, holding the letter with both hands, swaying back and forth in sorrow.

"Mordecai, look at me," ordered Ginzl.

She stood up. Though she towered above Mordecai ben Yahbahbai, huddled in a heap on the rock, weeping and moaning, her devotion and anger and determination made this tall woman even taller, made this strong woman even stronger, this lovely woman even more handsome.

"Look at me," she again commanded.

But he wouldn't lift his head.

Like a hawk swooping down on a hare, sinking its talons into the helpless little animal, and carrying it skyward, Ginzl grasped her husband by the lapels, stood him up, and pulled him so near that her face was very close to his.

"You must listen to me, my love," she said to him. "Stop crying and listen to me."

"I'm listening, my wonderful Ginzl," he answered, unsuccessfully trying to cease his weeping.

She put both her arms around him and held him like a baby. Looking at the clouds, framing her words carefully, his head on her shoulder, she spoke to him.

"Do you remember when we were in our first years of marriage before Liebeh was born and you and I went for outings on a lake—do you remember, my Mordecai?"

"I remember," he replied.

"There were snow geese on that lake. Do you remember the snow geese, Mordecai?"

"I remember the snow geese. When they were angry they honked and ruffled their neck feathers."

"Yes. Such funny fellows."

Mordecai ben Yahbahbai lifted his head and looked

into his wife's fine face. "Yes. Very comical, except when they chased me and tried to bite." He laughed through his tears.

Smiling, relieved that he seemed in better spirits, she put her hand behind his neck and gently guided his head until it again rested on her shoulder.

"When the snow geese flew above the lake, they were so beautiful," she said. "Their strong wings spread wide, lifting their bodies with such power. And sometimes they flew into the wind and hung in the sky, not moving, suspended, their wings out, their bodies still, floating and floating, as if they *belonged* in the sky, surrounded by only air. Such grace. Do you recall?"

"Yes, Ginzl. I recall."

"And then they landed on the water, these huge birds. They alighted so gently, the water hardly rippled. And when they swam, they were as beautiful as when they were flying—even when the water was still as glass, they hardly left any wavelets in their wakes—swimming with their heads high and necks so graceful, their bodies seemingly weightless, like fluff wafting in a breeze. Just as the snow geese were at home in the air, so were they at home in the water. They were unforgettable, flying above the lake, swimming in it."

"Yes. They were unforgettable."

"And then, my Mordecai, they came out of the water and walked on land." She laughed. "Do you recall?"

He raised his head and chuckled. "On land a snow goose is the clumsiest, most awkward, most bumbling, stumbling, gawkiest, least graceful creature on earth. On land a snow goose looks like a fat man on stilts. Any minute, he might fall over, like this—" And Mordecai ben Yahbahbai, to Ginzl's almost girlish delight, squatted and walked like a snow goose on land, flapping his elbows like wings.

"Yes. That's it. A goose waddles worse than a duck—that's it! that's it!—one leg going out this way, the other going out that way, beating his wings so he can keep his balance, his neck not knowing which way to go, one minute bent backward, the next minute straining forward as far as it can stretch."

"Yes." Mordecai ben Yahbahbai smiled, standing straight, a little out of breath from being a waterfowl. "Oh, yes. Especially when he runs, especially when he's angry and chasing somebody like me. And he bumps into other geese, as if he had had too much vodka," laughed Mordecai.

"Mordecai," said Ginzl, no longer laughing.

"Yes?" He looked into her eyes.

"You are a goose," she said.

"Yes. Just now, when I walked funny, I was being a goose."

"Not just now, Mordecai. Since we first saw each other, I thought you were a goose."

"I, a goose?"

"A snow goose."

"My love, you must tell me why."

"Because when you write your poems, or tell your wonderful stories to our children and our neighbors, you soar so gracefully, suspended, floating, surrounded by nothing but your imagination, free as a flying bird, like snow geese on the wing, and when you play your music and compose rhymes to the melodies, you are like the snow geese on water, so at home, weightless, peaceful, the picture of grace."

She paused and ruefully smiled.

"But—my Mordecai, when you are on land—in the world of reality, where there are no fairy tales and no beautiful music—you are also a goose. You bump into things. You don't know where you are going. You are very clumsy in the world of reality."

"I'm so sorry, my beloved Ginzl."

"I'm not," she quickly responded. "Is a snow goose perfect? No. Are you perfect? No. I knew that when I fell in love with you. I fell in love with you when you flew in the air and when you floated on the water—and I also loved you when you were on land. Alas, poor Mordecai, my sweet and strong and weak and hurtful husband, you rare man, your imagination and honesty and faith and logic make you unsuited for reality. You are terrible about money. Easy to cheat. Sometimes blind to others' needs. But land, sea, or air—I love you."

"Thank you, my Ginzele. I love you."

They kissed, a tender kiss, a long kiss, their lips barely touching, like a bumblebee gently hovering over a sweet flower.

For a moment neither spoke. Finally Ginzl said, "Mordecai, do you want to go to America?"

"More than anything. But now, how can we go?"

"What happened to your faith in the goodness of human beings?"

He thought for a few seconds, then shyly smiled and shrugged. "I still have it."

"Shimkeh said in his letter that there was still hope."

Mordecai ben Yahbahbai's smile became as bright as the sunlight. "Yes," he mused, "the letter said it might not be much longer. But, my Ginzl, do you believe it?"

"My faith is in you. The Mordecai I love would never stop hoping. He would never lose his faith."

"No! He wouldn't! I won't lose my faith!" exclaimed Mordecai ben Yahbahbai.

"We are going to America," said Ginzl.

"Yes!"

"Say it, Mordecai," she ordered.

"We are going to America!" exclaimed Mordecai ben Yahbahbai.

"Louder," she commanded.

His voice boomed out, over the brook, through the trees, into the sky.

"Some day—one day—WE ARE GOING TO AMERICA!"

"Yes!" she whispered. "Now, Mordecai, let's return to the house and tell the children you have faith."

"Right away!" said Mordecai ben Yahbahbai. Quickly, he started toward home.

"Mordecai!"

He stopped and turned.

"Yes, my beloved?"

"Wait for me."

11

A FEW weeks later on a balmy Sabbath afternoon beneath a cloudless April sky, Yuri, Liebeh, and Dovidl sat around the table in Yuri's log cabin. Shafts of glittering spring light shone boldly through the windows, penetrating the darkness inside the small dwelling, brightening the humble house, making its scant, rough-hewn furnishings seem less shabby and forbidding.

Just outside, on a variety of benches and stools, Yuri's elderly parents and his sisters, their faces to the sunbeams sifting down through the surrounding trees, rested from their arduous labors and restored themselves so they would be strong enough to face the week ahead.

Inside the log cabin Yuri showed Dovidl how to make a fishing lure from thread and feathers. The boy's eyes hardly left the young man's hands as Yuri trimmed the feather before he tied it to an ancient fishhook.

Liebeh, however, seemed unusually subdued. She watched motes of dust dance in the brilliance of the sunlight, but her concentration was inward. Occasionally Yuri glanced up at her from his fishhook-making and they exchanged unspoken, sad looks.

Finally, as if forcing herself to join the two males' preoccupation, she asked, "Why do you need a feather?"

"Why do we need a feather, Dovidl?" Yuri demanded from Dovidl, as a mentor might examine his apprentice.

"To make the fish think the fishhook is a bug. To make the lure wiggle and dart through the water. To make the trout chase it," recited Dovidl.

"He learns well, that brother of yours," praised Yuri, beaming.

"Dovidl, why don't you go to the brook and try the new lure?" prompted Liebeh. "Go and fish. Bring home a trout for dinner."

"That isn't such a good idea today," Yuri said.

"Why?" queried Liebeh.

"The Czar's game warden has been seen around here. Dovidl doesn't know where the safe places are, hidden shores of the brook the game warden wouldn't think to patrol," Yuri explained.

"I don't understand," Liebeh mused. "Why would the game warden prevent a little boy from fishing?"

For the first time since he'd known Yuri, Dovidl saw an angry flush redden the young man's fair complexion.

His eyes flashing with resentment but his voice remaining even and quiet, Yuri stood up and said through clenched teeth, "Oh, the game warden wouldn't *prevent* a little boy from fishing, Liebeh. The game warden would *shoot* the little boy. Or, if the boy is lucky, the game warden would just arrest him and send him to the Czar's workhouse for children."

"But why, Yuri?" Liebeh asked.

"Because the fish belong to the Czar," Yuri growled. "The brook belongs to the Czar. The forest belongs to the Czar. In this forest everything—and everyone—belongs to the Czar. When we are hungry and the deer come up to our gardens and eat the young ears of corn before they can be harvested, may we kill the deer and have venison to eat along with our corn? No. The deer belong to the Czar. When the children go into the forest and gather wild strawberries and almonds fallen from the trees, they are in danger of their lives. The fruits and nuts belong to the Czar. Taking anything from the Czar's forest is punishable by death."

"I've never seen the game warden around here," said Dovidl.

"This is a small place," Yuri replied. "He usually doesn't bother us. But around us serfs have been murdered for poaching and their houses and churches burned down by the Czar's agents—those rotten cossacks and that blood-loving game warden. I have spoken to the sons of murdered fathers. One day, if someone catches the game warden alone in the forest, and no one is watching—" Yuri slapped his huge fist into his open palm.

"Yuri, don't be so angry," Liebeh said. "Finish the fishing lure."

"Yes," he answered. Sitting down and resuming his task, he said, "Forgive me."

Liebeh touched him on the arm and whispered, "We understand. I feel as you do."

Dovidl watched Liebeh and Yuri exchange a look of compassion, loving and yet subdued. "Why are they so unhappy today?" he thought. "When I find the right girl for me, I won't be melancholy."

Impulsively, he blurted, "If I were in love, I wouldn't be sad."

"Dovidl!" Liebeh exclaimed. "Who said we were in love?"

"Everyone." Dovidl grinned. "Even a touched-in-the-head simpleton would know. You and Yuri are always sighing and giggling at each other. Why don't you get married?"

"You be quiet, Dovidl ben Mordecai, or I'll—I'll—!"

"Liebeh, please." Yuri laughed. "It's true, Dovidl. Everyone knows how we feel about each other and that we want to get married." He paused and his grin faded into a frown. "Everyone except—"

"Everyone except who?" Dovidl pressed.

"Never mind!" cried Liebeh.

"Yes, Dovidl," said Yuri, manfully giving Dovidl a shove on the shoulder. "Never mind. Forget it." And the young man again began shaping the lure.

Mentally shrugging, Dovidl again concentrated on Yuri's busy fingers, ignoring Liebeh, who glared upward at the dark rafters.

After a few moments, however, the boy said, "I wonder if they have trout in America."

"Why?" snapped Liebeh. "You're never going there."

"Oh, yes," said Dovidl, quietly but firmly. "We're all going to America. Papa says so."

"Oh, Dovidl," derided Liebeh. "Do you really believe Shimkeh will get passports for us?"

"Yes," Dovidl answered.

"Well, I don't. And I'm glad. I don't want to go to America."

Reluctantly, Dovidl turned his attention away from Yuri's deft hands and stared at his sister.

"Why don't you want to go to America?" he asked.

"Because," Liebeh said, her lovely eyes fixed on Yuri's face, "I like it very much right here where we are."

Yuri paused in his task and she and he silently drank of each other.

"Phooey," said Dovidl. "Papa wrote to Shimkeh and told him to bring the passports and not to come here without them. Therefore, since Shimkeh wants to come here, he'll bring the passports. That's logic."

"Oh, Dovidl"—Liebeh sighed—"stop trying to sound like Papa. Shimkeh is in trouble. He wants to hide here. Here's what Papa told him in the letter: sometimes there are cossacks in this place. And I say that if there are cossacks here, Shimkeh *won't* come. *That's* logic. Now you and Yuri go fishing."

"Let's all go fishing," Yuri said. "We'll try this lure and see how it works. We'll catch enough of the Czar's trout for my parents' table and yours as well. Come, Liebeh."

Once more Liebeh and Yuri exchanged a look of love mixed with sadness.

"No, thank you. I have other things to do," she said to him sweetly. "I'm going home. Mama might need help with the children."

"Now," Liebeh said to her brother, "you and Yuri go fishing."

GINZL didn't need help with the children. Her infants napped soundly in their cribs and the older babies played just outside the door under the watchful care of eight-year-old Fraydl. Meanwhile, Mordecai ben Yahbahbai was taking his afternoon walk in the forest, thinking and humming and having discussions with himself.

Sitting at the table having a peaceful glass of tea, Ginzl and Yosip the Baker gazed out the open windows and gloried in the gentleness of this rare April day. After a while, however, her attention strayed from the window and she began studying the old man's kind face.

Aware that she was looking at him, Yosip smiled at her and said, "Yes, Ginzl?"

"Yes, what, my dear Yosip?"

"You are just like Liebeh. When she looks at me as you are looking, I know that very soon a question is coming my way."

"Perhaps it's a question I have no right to ask."

"You may ask of me whatever you wish. What is the question?"

"Why are you in this place? How did you come here? Everyone, except for you, is a peasant, a laborer. You are a man of some education, born in the city, a master baker, so different from the people here."

"The answer"—Yosip smiled—"is short and long, sad and sweet, very reasonable and completely unreasonable. When I was a young man in the city, I could not find a wife. Oh, how I wanted someone to love and make a home for, who would bear us sons and daughters. But somehow all the women I liked were spoken for, and all the women who liked me, I didn't care for. All the while, since I owned my own bakery, I had money. So I went shopping. I bought a wife."

He studied Ginzl's face. "You are not disgusted?"

"I never pass judgment on those I love. Go ahead, Yosip."

"I found a very poor farmer with many daughters. I chose the smartest and prettiest one, gave her father gold, and she and I were wed. We were very happy. She was a wonderful girl." He sighed, then laughed sadly. "Our marriage lasted one year." His eyes became blank, as if they were focusing on something in the past, something so painful that he was afraid to allow it to show on his face. His voice became very quiet. "There was an epidemic. Many died. One morning my beautiful, childlike wife was fine. By nightfall, she was gone."

"Oh, Yosip."

He shrugged. "It was a lifetime ago. The wound has healed. But I thought then—I think now—she would be alive today had I not been so selfish and taken her from the farm to a crowded, dirty city." Stroking his white beard, he said ruefully, "When she died, I cut myself off from my friends and family. I joined the army. And when I finished being a soldier, I looked for a place to do penance—I looked for the most isolated, loneliest spot I could find. A place where nobody stopped." He laughed. "Because there were restaurants and food markets in Vitebsk and Smolensk who still remembered my baking, I had no trouble getting customers and supplying them by stagecoach. So I came here and lived alone, cried alone, drank alone, worked alone, for twenty-five long years. Until you and your husband and Liebeh came."

A sad grin spread across Yosip the Baker's face. "And do you know why my story is so unreasonable?"

Ginzl smiled back. "Yes," she said. "You, who wanted to get away from everybody, who wanted to be alone, you, my dear Yosip the Baker, love people and companionship more than anyone I have ever known."

"And look where I found love and companionship." Again, he chuckled. "In the place where nobody stops."

"Yes," said Ginzl, also laughing. But after a moment, a strange and searching expression altered her smile. In fact, she seemed so lost in what she was thinking, she didn't notice that Liebeh had appeared at the open door behind her.

"Yosip, my friend, both our lives were shaped by forces over which we had no control," said Ginzl. "If not for a large bar of soap, I never would have married Mordecai ben Yahbahbai."

Liebeh put a finger to her lips, so that Yosip would not let Ginzl know her daughter was listening, eager to hear.

"A bar of soap?" repeated Yosip, raising his eyebrows in surprise.

"A very *large* bar of soap," said Ginzl, smiling.

Yosip directed an almost imperceptible wink toward Liebeh to let her know he wouldn't betray her presence and then said to Ginzl, "Tell me about the bar of soap."

"When I was a maiden," Ginzl began, "I was courted by many men. My father was quite pleased. The one man he disliked, however, was my Mordecai. Mordecai ben Yahbahbai was a highly regarded young teacher in a boys' school, but my father absolutely forbade me to see him."

Even though he thought he knew the answer, Yosip laughed and asked, "And why did your father dislike him so?"

"Because Mordecai ben Yahbahbai questioned everything. He questioned the old ways. He questioned the new ways. If you gave him an answer, he questioned the answer. If you asked him a question, he questioned the question. Anything, everything, Mordecai ben Yahbahbai questioned it. On the other hand, my father was a very traditional man. He questioned nothing. So the very mention of Mordecai's name sent my father into a terrible rage. Mordecai knew this. But Mordecai being Mordecai, he came to our front door and questioned why my father would not receive him. Well, my father was also a man of much determination. He told the maid to go upstairs to the balcony and empty a pail of water on Mordecai's head. The maid forgot that there was a heavy bar of soap in the bucket.

"The bar of soap almost knocked my poor Mordecai unconscious. They brought him into the house, and while he questioned why anyone would hit him with a bar of soap, and while my mother attended to the bump on his head, Mordecai and I fell in love." Ginzl laughed. "He told me that falling in love with me was the first thing in his life he didn't question." After a moment, Ginzl added, "A few years later, I asked Mordecai, 'Why don't you question anything anymore?' He said, 'There's no need. Since I fell in love with you and our Liebeh was born, I know the answers to the important questions, and who has time to waste on unimportant questions?' "

From behind Ginzl, Liebeh whispered, "Mama, I heard what you said."

Startled, Ginzl rose and stared at her lovely daughter.

"You said that your father didn't want you to marry Papa," whispered Liebeh.

"Yes," Ginzl sighed, after a moment.

"Then you understand how I feel. Why don't you help me with Papa?" she asked. "Oh, Mama! *Your* Papa! *My* Papa! Do they think they own us? I'm sixteen, Mama. I'm a woman. I'm in love with a fine young man. Why won't Papa talk to him?"

"Papa talks to him. Yuri asks Papa more questions than anyone else when Papa is telling his stories."

"I don't mean questions about Napoleon or the Statue of Liberty or what makes a balloon fly, questions in front of a roomful of people. Why won't Papa talk to Yuri in private—about *me*?"

It took Ginzl a moment to phrase her answer. "Liebeh, my love, Papa thinks Yuri is not the right kind of young man for you."

"Is it because Yuri is not of our faith?"

"No. Your father is an enlightened and modern man."

With an odd smile, Liebeh asked, "Then is it because Yuri is an uneducated woodchopper?"

When Ginzl did not answer, Liebeh said with pride, "Yuri has a fine mind, Mama. You'd be surprised and pleased. He's very intelligent." Liebeh took her mother's hand. "Speak to Papa, Mama. Tell him to sit with Yuri and talk to him and get to know him."

"I already did. Papa refuses."

Surprised, Liebeh asked, "You did?" She raised her arms to heaven, just as her father did when life was beyond comprehension. "Won't *anybody* help me? Doesn't he know how I feel? Oh, I'm so angry, Mama. My father brought me to a place where there are only woodchoppers—yet he doesn't want me to marry a woodchopper. What does he expect me to do, marry a pine tree?" Liebeh stamped her foot. "It's all Papa's fault, giving Shimkeh money, waiting here for ten years, knowing Shimkeh will never come. Papa does such foolish things. How can you love such a man?"

"Liebeh!" Yosip the Baker gasped. "He's your father. You're his life."

"It's all right, Yosip," said Ginzl softly.

To Liebeh she said, "How can I love such a man? Because he has the soul of a poet. When one falls in love with a man who does foolish things, it's better if he has the soul of a poet. Then the foolishness is bearable."

Liebeh began to sob.

"Come. Come to your mama, my child," Ginzl said. She opened her arms to Liebeh.

Liebeh ran to Ginzl and clung to her. "Mama, I didn't mean what I said. I love Papa so. Oh, help me, Mama. Tell Papa to talk to Yuri."

12

SO, for the first time in ten years, unhappiness invaded Yosip the Baker's house and refused to go away.

Liebeh cried because she was in love but could not marry. Ginzl cried because Liebeh cried. All the other children—Dovidl, Fraydl, Deeneh, Ya'akov, Moishl, Ahvrom Tevyeh, Boruch, Simchl, Timmeh Layeh, and Rochl—cried because Liebeh and Ginzl cried. And Mordecai ben Yahbahbai cried more loudly and more often than anyone, not only because everyone in his family cried, but because the noise of all that crying kept him from sleeping each day until noon.

As for Yosip the Baker, his heart, which had been light and happy so much of the time during the past ten years, became as heavy as a sponge in a sea of tears.

THE two men measured each other—Mordecai ben Yahbahbai, a wiry, tiny man whose center of existence was in his heart and mind, and Yuri, tall and muscled, a man who worked with his body—and Mordecai ben Yahbahbai was absolutely certain they had nothing in common except that they both loved Liebeh.

Yuri took off his cap and said, "Thank you for seeing me, sir."

"Don't thank me. Seeing you was not my idea," replied Mordecai ben Yahbahbai.

"No, kind sir. I mean, yes, kind sir." Yuri shifted his feet uncomfortably.

Spring had almost spent itself and summer was coming. They were alone in the house. Everyone else—Ginzl and the children, Yosip the Baker, an apprehensive Liebeh—ate Sunday lunch at an outdoor table behind the cottage.

Mordecai ben Yahbahbai cleared his throat and chose his words carefully. "In all the years we've been married, my wife has never insisted on anything. Now, all of a sudden, she insists. She insists that I talk to you about my Liebeh. Very well, I'm talking to you about my Liebeh. I'm against it. I'm against it. I'm against it." Mordecai ben Yahbahbai paused. "Do you understand what I just said?"

"I understand, sir," answered Yuri. "You're against it. You don't want Liebeh to marry me."

"Excellent. We're off to a very good start."

"With respect, sir, may I ask why you're against our marrying?"

"There are several reasons, all having to do with logic. First, I've no money for a dowry. I paid my life's savings—ninety rubles and ten kopeks—to my cousin Shimkeh, who is using the money to get passports so that my family can go to America. Therefore, aside from not having a dowry, logic tells me that when Shimkeh *does* come with the passports, Liebeh can't stay here with you and go to America with me at the same time.

"Third, and this is the most logical reason of all, my daughter is an educated young woman. She helps me teach all her brothers and sisters. She reads my books and we discuss them.

"On the other hand, you have no education. Do you think all there is to marriage is kissing and loving? Kissing and loving do not take up a great deal of time. Afterward, when you're tired of kissing and loving, what will you talk about? How can the two of you look at the world in the same way? She's not of your faith. What mutual interests have you? Logic tells me the answer is none—you have nothing in common. It would be a disaster. So thank you for coming, young man. Good-bye."

"But, sir," said Yuri, "may I not say anything to you? You've given me all your reasons why not. I've good reasons why yes."

"I promised that I'd listen," sighed Mordecai ben Yahbahbai. "So sit. And talk. I'm listening."

"Thank you, sir." Yuri sat at the table across from Mordecai ben Yahbahbai, fixed his eyes on the older man with great purpose, and began to speak, quietly at first, but with increasing confidence and force.

"First of all, kind sir, the dowry makes no difference to us. Liebeh and I believe that people in love needn't buy each other. Second, if you go to America, perhaps Liebeh and I would also go to America. Or, perhaps we wouldn't. We're free to do as we wish. Respectfully, sir, it's our life, not yours. Third, yes, she's not of my faith, but I know from your teachings that you believe this is a time of liberation, a time of freedom and new ideas."

Yuri sat up even straighter and his voice strengthened. "And lastly, yes, it's true—I work with my hands. I chop wood—wood that builds libraries, wood that makes the paper for the books in those libraries, wood that makes tablets for you to write on, wood that keeps people warm during the winter and heats ovens for baking bread. There's no dishonor in chopping wood—in working with the hands. Every bite of bread Yosip the Baker bakes has been kneaded and shaped by his two good hands."

"Yes," replied Mordecai ben Yahbahbai, "there's great honor in work. But bees and ants and oxen work. You're not an insect or a beast of the field. You're a man and there's more to a man than work, than muscles. A man also has a brain."

"Liebeh told me you would say that, sir, and I agree with you. But I assure you, I have a brain. It's because of you that I am learning to use it."

"Because of me?"

"Yes, kind sir. Just as you taught Liebeh to read and write, she has taught me."

With a triumphant light in his eyes, Yuri took a stack of worn pamphlets from his pocket. "I earned these from a peddler in exchange for fixing his wagon. Choose one, sir, and I'll read for you."

Mordecai ben Yahbahbai, without looking, chose one of the pamphlets, thrust it toward the young man, and quietly said, "My small sons and daughters also read for me. They know how to put the sounds of the letters together until the sounds make a word. The problem is, most of the time they don't understand what the word means. So you're able to read words. Congratulations. But do you understand what the words mean?"

Not affronted by Mordecai ben Yahbahbai and nodding his head in agreement, Yuri replied quite seriously, "I try very hard to understand what I'm reading, kind sir."

Following cach word with his index finger, his voice firm and confident, Yuri read from the pamphlet: " 'I sit on a man's back, choking him and making him carry me, and yet assure myself and others that I am very sorry for him and wish to ease his lot by all possible means—except by getting off his back.' "

Surprised, Mordecai ben Yahbahbai whispered, "Tolstoy." Nodding, impressed despite himself, he smiled at Yuri. "And what else do you read?"

"Anything. I read every night by candlelight. Pamphlets, borrowed books, old newspapers, the holy Bible, whatever I can find to read. Liebeh and I read to each other. We talk about the meaning of what we read."

"And what do you plan to do with all this reading?"

"Whatever we decide. We've made no plans, sir, other than to spend our lives together. Perhaps we'll stay here, in this place. Perhaps we'll go to the city, to Vitebsk or Smolensk, and see how it is there, see what we can learn, what we can do to help make the world better. Or perhaps we'll go to America. The main thing is, please, sir, we wish to marry." After a pause, Yuri asked, "May we have your blessing?"

Liebeh's father stood up, went to the window, turning his back on Yuri, and had a silent conversation with himself. Since he did not want Yuri to know what he was thinking, and since he spoke with his hands as much

---

Sitting on the shelf was a partially wrapped object, the loosened ribbon around it still dangling.

as with his tongue, Mordecai ben Yahbahbai kept those expressive hands of his firmly clasped behind his back.

Nonetheless, Mordecai ben Yahbahbai's face revealed his thoughts. One eyebrow went up. His mouth turned down into a frown. He shook his head from side to side. He twitched his nose and pursed his lips. After a moment, the other eyebrow went down, and all the wrinkles in his face deepened. Then he slowly turned his head and raised his eyebrows, while his gaze focused on a shelf across the room.

Sitting on the shelf was a partially wrapped object, the loosened ribbon around the package still dangling. Only two people in the world knew what lay inside the wrapping. The day before, Liebeh had given the parcel to him. Thinking it was a gift, Mordecai ben Yahbahbai opened it with pomp and a flourish, then stared at the contents, puzzled at first, then looking up incredulously at his bright-eyed daughter. Inside the package was a large cake of soap. Wordlessly, Liebeh had stared at him for a moment and then turned away and gone about her business.

Mordecai ben Yahbahbai, momentarily transfixed by the package on the shelf, gradually turned his eyes away and looked out the window. He watched Liebeh for a moment, standing in the sunlight beneath a canopy of new spring leaves, this young woman who had been his infant baby, his lovely headstrong child, his beautiful daughter grown into a rare and fine human being—and slowly the wrinkles in his face vanished. The frown transformed itself into a look of acceptance, and he began to nod his head up and down. Reluctantly, Mordecai ben Yahbahbai was agreeing with himself.

Turning to Yuri, he said softly, "It's not easy for a

father to give away his daughter in marriage. Liebeh doesn't want to lose you and I don't want to lose Liebeh. And I also wish to avoid the mistakes of the past."

"I swear I'll love and protect her, kind sir."

"Yes, Yuri. I'm sure of it."

Putting his hand paternally on the young man's broad shoulder, Mordecai ben Yahbahbai, nodding soberly, said, "I like you, my son. You have my blessing."

13

ONE June morning a few weeks later, Yuri and his fellow woodchoppers, as they did each day, made their way deep into the Czar's forest.

It was an hour before dawn. The night sky was at its blackest. But even in the darkness, Yuri and the other men of the place where nobody stopped knew every inch of every path and trail in the forest. It was their home.

As they marched to work, they sang in their deep and booming voices,

"In the summer we burn; in the winter we freeze;
We spend all our lives felling the trees."

But although chopping wood for the Czar was back-breaking and dangerous and barely paid a man enough to feed his family, Yuri loved the forest. He treasured the deep, perfumed carpet of pine needles beneath his boots. High, high above, the topmost branches of majestic oaks and cedars were like the quiet ceiling of a cathedral whose stained-glass windows filtered and softened the sunlight. Busy squirrels and chipmunks scampered to and fro, up and down, all around. Shy deer, the color of faded autumn leaves, stood motionless in the shadows and watched Yuri at work. Occasionally, an ursine shadow clambered through the brush, Ivan the big-footed Russian bear, running from the sight and smell of man.

But most of all, Yuri cherished the *silence* of the forest. Except for the echoing, thumping whack-whacks of axes biting into wood, except for warning shouts of "Timber!" when a tree was about to fall, except for the groaning of the huge trunk as it teetered and the earth-shaking explosion as it crashed to the ground, except for the rasping of handsaws trimming the branches from the huge trunk as it lay wounded on the forest floor, except for the grunting of the men as they chained the trunk to a team of oxen to be dragged to the river and floated downstream to the Czar's lumber mill—except for these sounds, all muted by the vastness of the forest, the woodland was a hushed place. Even the woodchoppers toiled in silence. Everyone knew what was required of him. There was no need for words. The men seldom spoke.

So this particular morning, Yuri was quite surprised when a group of his fellow woodchoppers came to talk to him.

Their spokesman was Uncle Oleg. When Oleg spoke, his neighbors paid attention. Oh, but people should only listen to me like that.

"Yuri, my lad," said Oleg, "we have talked among ourselves. Now we wish to talk to you."

Bewildered, Yuri leaned his ax against a tree, wiped the perspiration from his face, and said, "Of course, Oleg my uncle."

"As you know, our fathers, and their fathers before them, worked all their lives in this forest," Oleg continued. "When their days were over, they had no more than when they were born—a hut to live and die in, rags to wear, a few potatoes and beets for the stomachs of their families."

"Yes," nodded Yuri, sadly, "that is true."

"We are as poor as our ancestors were. Nothing has changed."

Again, gravely, Yuri agreed. "That is also true. Nothing has changed."

"So this is what we have decided," said Oleg. "We want a school for our children."

Even though he did not smile, Yuri was pleased. "Yes. I agree," he replied.

"Good. If our children have a school, perhaps some of them will have a chance to live better lives."

"Yes," said Yuri, quietly. He looked each man in the eye. "I am with you. What must I do, my brethren?"

"Go to Yosip the Baker and Mordecai ben Yahbahbai. You will soon be part of their family. Speak for us. Tell them that even though we have no money, we will build a schoolhouse with what God gave us—wood and stone and strong muscles.

"Tell them we want Mordecai ben Yahbahbai to be our schoolmaster and enlighten our children, just as he has enlightened all of us for these ten years past.

"Tell them that we have no money to pay Mordecai ben Yahbahbai for being our schoolmaster. Instead of money, we will pay him by building a room in the schoolhouse for his daughter Liebeh and you to live in when you are married."

After a pause, Yuri said, "I thank you, but Liebeh

and I do not need help. We want only what we earn."

Smiling, Oleg answered, "You will earn it. Liebeh will help her father teach our children."

For a moment, Yuri thought about Oleg's proposal, then replied, "I must ask Liebeh."

"Yes," said Oleg. "And if she agrees?"

Yuri grinned. "Then I also agree."

"Good," said Oleg.

The older man spat on the calloused palm of his right hand and held it out to Yuri, who also spat on the palm of his strong hand.

Resolutely, the two men shook hands to seal their understanding and then went back to work.

YURI and Liebeh, standing very close together in front of the big stone oven, told Yosip the Baker, Mordecai ben Yahbahbai, and Ginzl what Oleg said.

When they finished, Liebeh asked, "Papa? What are your feelings in this matter?"

For a few seconds Mordecai ben Yahbahbai tugged on his beard, nodded and shook his head, had a brief debate with himself, then replied, "Before I give my answer, I want to know what Mama's feelings are."

"It's a wonderful idea, my Mordecai. It would be a blessing," said Ginzl. "But be warned, my love—" she added, smiling—"you would have to rise *early* each morning."

"Aha," replied Mordecai ben Yahbahbai, inspecting the floor. "Early, eh?"

"And you would be too tired to tell your stories to our neighbors each night," Ginzl continued.

"Too tired, eh?" mused Mordecai ben Yahbahbai, holding his hands behind him and swaying to and fro.

"But Papa," Liebeh chimed in, "once a week, perhaps each Saturday night, we could still meet and listen to you."

"Once a week, eh?" her father echoed. He pulled his ear and scratched his nose.

"And I'd be there every morning at the school, waiting for you. And we'd work together all day, you and I."

"Aha," said Mordecai ben Yahbahbai thoughtfully. "That sounds very nice." Turning to Yosip the Baker, he asked, "And what do you think, our dear friend?"

Yosip the Baker pondered for a moment, then put his hands under his belly, pushed upward until his chest stuck out, and said, "Mordecai ben Yahbahbai, the people of this place are deeply in your debt. Who brought us pleasure and inspiration? You, my oldest and closest friend. Now, if you teach our children, we shall be even further in your debt." He paused. "Do I want you to do this thing? Yes, I do. It is not, however, for me to decide. *You* must decide."

Mordecai ben Yahbahbai went to his window and consulted the clouds. Whenever he thought profound thoughts, he liked to look at the sky, as if four walls were too small an area in which to make great decisions. And there he stood, debating inside himself, questioning, questioning, questioning.

Every eye in the room was fixed on Mordecai ben Yahbahbai. For a moment, it was very quiet. Even the babies sensed something unusual and stopped their jabbering and gurgling and cooing and watched their father.

Finally, the dialogue inside him concluded, Mordecai ben Yahbahbai turned to them and said, simply, "My loved ones, I have always been a teacher. I was born to be a teacher. So now, instead of teaching just my own children, I shall teach our neighbors' children as well. And our Liebeh, by helping me, will earn a place to live in the bargain."

And here, suddenly, Mordecai ben Yahbahbai pointed his finger toward the sky and proclaimed, loudly, "*But!* And this is a very *big but*."

Mordecai ben Yahbahbai swept the room with his eyes, gazing at each of them in turn.

"*But!*" he said. "When Shimkeh comes with the passports, we are going to America."

14

AS we all know, everything always happened the same way in the place where nobody stopped.

But now, in this summer of 1906, everything began to happen for either the first time—or the last time.

It was the third day of the seventh month, the date on which the Sergeant Major and his cossacks swept through the countryside between Vitebsk and Smolensk in search of recruits for the glorious army of the Czar.

But after having served his Czar and Mother Russia all his adult life, the Sergeant Major was drawing near the end of his military career. This year would be his final tour of duty. Today would be the last time he would ever ride through the place where nobody stopped.

Even though he was as tall and fierce-looking as ever, lately small afflictions had begun to distress him. Last winter gray hairs appeared in his ink black, waxed mustache. Since the weather was cold, he successfully colored the silver strands with black boot polish. Now, however, in the heat of July the waxy polish liquefied and ran down his chin. Fortunately, he discovered the dark streaks in the mirror before any of his men noticed.

Also, his eyes now failed him in the strangest ways. One year ago today, the last time he punished Yosip the Baker, as he beat and kicked the stubborn old fool, he noticed that the round little man looked like a kindly priest, or someone's genial uncle, or a biblical prophet—or, strangest of all, one of the seraphim in the oil paintings in the St. Petersburg museum. Since then, as the Sergeant Major administered punishment, his eyes continued to betray him. Instead of disobedient dogs who deserved all the pain he could give them, he saw his victims as merely men, with bodies and souls the same as his.

And not only did his eyes deceive him, but his hearing began to trick him as well. His captives' cries and laments and moans and wails, which had never before affected him one way or another, now pained his ears until his head ached. On such occasions, the Sergeant Major whipped off his silk scarf, wiped his eyes so he could see more clearly, cleaned out his ears so he could hear more acutely, and, cursing to himself, ordered one of his men to finish the punishment while he walked his horse far enough away from the scene of the beating so he could neither see nor hear the slashing whip and the screams.

This morning, before he left his quarters in the barracks, the Sergeant Major opened a bureau drawer and took out a small box wrapped in oily brown paper. Over the bureau hung a mirror, and he forced himself to examine his face in it. Sure enough, another gray hair had appeared in his mustache. Angrily, he plucked it out, strapped on his sword, donned his plumed silver helmet, and, carrying the small box wrapped in oily brown paper, strode outside to the parade grounds, where his platoon awaited him at attention.

Before he approached his own horse, the Sergeant Major stepped in front of a young corporal and said, "Since you are to replace me soon, today I shall teach you a valuable lesson—how to discipline rebellious scum. A peasant is like a horse. He may be taught in three ways. Sometimes by using the whip, other times by giving him sugar, and, the best way, by using both the whip and the sugar together, without letting him know which it will be. Before this day is done, you will see what I mean."

"Yes, your Excellency," snapped the young corporal, saluting smartly.

The Sergeant Major swaggered to his horse, steadied the huge, wild-eyed charger by affectionately but sharply slapping it on the side of its neck, and stuffed the box wrapped in oily brown paper into his saddlebag. Grandly, he mounted the beast, stood tall in the stirrups, drew his sword, pointed it toward the stockade gate, bellowed, "Platoon, forward," dug his spurs into the horse's flanks, and, in a whirlwind of dust and an earthquake of hooves, wildly led his platoon of cossacks out of the fortress.

AT about the same time, Oleg walked along the road toward Smolensk. He'd left home in the black of predawn. Now his long-striding, strong legs ate up the distance as he marched purposefully forward, and even though the dusty road sweltered in the July heat, by midmorning he reached his destination, a small, unpretentious, unpainted wooden church on the outskirts of the city.

Without hesitating, Oleg walked through the gate of

the low, weathered picket fence that ran around the yard and cemetery. He stepped aside and made way for the worshipers leaving the church after Sunday mass. At the door, a priest spoke to each of his flock as he or she emerged. The churchman had a full gray beard and wore a tall black satin hat, a dark flowing robe that reached the floor, and, around his neck, a heavy crucifix on a long, thick gold chain.

When the last person had departed and the priest was about to go back into the church, Oleg called, "Father Nikolai? Father Nikolai?"

Furrowing his brows in surprise, Father Nikolai said, "Oleg, my son. Why are you here? Is there trouble in your home?"

TWENTY miles to the west, traveling on their way from Vitebsk toward the place where nobody stopped, two women, one tall and very beautiful, the other squatty and very ugly, their babushkas almost covering their faces, also made their way along our road in a creaky, broken-down buggy pulled by a balky, bewhiskered old horse who could barely walk, much less trot or run. The unattractive woman smoked a cigar.

"Are you hot, my dear?" the short woman, who was Shimkeh in a dress, asked the tall woman.

The tall woman, Froomeh, wrinkled her lovely face, searching for an answer. Finally she said, "Yes."

"Would you like some water, my flower, my diamond, my only love?"

She thought about it and again said, "Yes."

"I wish I had some to give you. Alas, my sun and moon and stars, when I, uh, purchased this buggy, I was in such a hurry to leave that I forgot to look and see if it had a water bag or canteen in it. Somewhere ahead, I pray, we'll come to a river or stream and we'll drink then."

As they rode through the heat, he chewed on his cigar and his eyes shifted from side to side, never still for a second, back and forth like the pendulum on a grandfather clock. He scanned the fields, the woods, the meadows, watching for danger, ever alert, his feet always moving in tiny nervous jig steps that made the rickety conveyance sway even more. Horrible scenarios passed through his mind like thunderclouds driven by a gale. Was that a cossack behind those trees? A gendarme hiding among those boulders? A policeman astride the oncoming roan? A government agent in the carriage that had just passed?

"Go faster, horse!" he commanded the old nag.

The swaybacked beast did not alter its slow walk, but it did turn its head toward Shimkeh and snort.

Shimkeh, wishing he had a buggy whip—there had been none when he appropriated the unguarded wagon from in front of a hospital—reached under his dress, removed his belt from his trousers, and doubled it, preparing to spur the venerable equine on.

But as he raised his arm and leaned forward to strike the horse's rump, Froomeh said, "Shimkeh?"

Traveling toward the place where nobody stopped, two women made their way along the road.

"Yes, the center of my universe, what is it?"

"Are you going to hit it?"

After the slightest of pauses, Shimkeh replied, "Oh, no. There's a fly on his rear. I was going to gently brush it away so the poor old thing wouldn't be so tormented. I? Hit an animal? Never!"

Froomeh smiled her vacant smile and leaned down and kissed Shimkeh's cheek.

"Thank you, my queen, my Czarina, my Mona Lisa," Shimkeh said to her.

To the horse he said, "Go faster, horse. *Please!*"

The horse didn't go faster.

MORDECAI ben Yahbahbai, sitting half-awake at the open window, looked outside and sleepily admired the summer morning. All around him, romping like puppies, his children played hide-and-seek under his chair, crawled on and off his lap, sang songs in his ear, danced on the table, or noisily helped Ginzl and Liebeh cook and clean.

But on beautiful days such as this, Mordecai ben Yahbahbai had the rare ability to hear only what he wished to hear. He ignored the happy noises of the children inside the house. Instead, his ears and drowsy mind acknowledged the music of nature outside the window, a symphony of whistling robins, scolding jays, nattering squirrels, the sudden snap and whirr of a diving hummingbird's wings, the penetrating drone of honeybees swarming among the wildflowers.

Just as he was about to nod off into a sweet, sun-kissed summer dream, however, a discordant note—huh? eh? what? who?—intruded itself into his consciousness. What was it? What? A crow? A cricket? A sudden wind rushing through the trees? What? What was this deep and annoying and alien and low-pitched yappety-yippety-yappety-yuppety? Why was it so persistent? And why was it so very angry?

Wakening, searching for the source of this desecration of such a beautiful July morning, Mordecai ben Yahbahbai peered out the window. At first glance everything seemed normal—the woods, the animal pens, the gardens. But the unidentifiable noise persisted. Sighing, he reluctantly rose from his chair and went outside to investigate.

The sounds seemed to be coming from the edge of the forest. Now fully awake, his interest as always sharpened by anything he did not understand, he walked faster as the noises increased and the mystery deepened. Ears cocked, he followed the sunlit path past the chicken coop, the woodshed, the garden, the vineyard, the cow pen, and, finally, to the beginning of the woods, where the brightness dimmed into cool shade.

With each step, the strange sounds grew louder, until Mordecai ben Yahbahbai realized that what he was hearing was a man's voice—an angry man's voice—arguing, shouting, ranting, chanting, raving, scolding, stuttering, muttering, sputtering, stammering, yammering. Seldom had he heard a person speak with such vehemence and passion.

Perhaps an insane inmate had escaped from an asylum and hidden himself in the place where nobody stopped. Even though he was a bit frightened, Mordecai ben Yahbahbai dropped to his hands and knees and crept nearer and nearer, until he was close enough to hear the rough panting of the speaker as he shouted and yawped.

Rising to his knees, Mordecai ben Yahbahbai peered between two bushes, and when he saw what he saw, his hand went to his heart, his mouth gaped in amazement, his eyes widened in shock and sorrow, and, to himself, he moaned, "Oh, no! Yosip the Baker has gone crazy! He is now a lunatic! His hard life has scrambled his mind and turned him into a crackbrain! And it's my fault. If not for me, the Sergeant Major never would have knocked him loose from his senses!"

Yosip the Baker, red-faced with fury, his eyes bulging, the veins in his neck sticking out like knotty ropes, screamed at the trees in an abnormal, high voice: "And someone should take a pitchfork and stick it into your front until it comes out your back! Then someone should take a heavy ax and split you open like a watermelon!"

Because he had no teeth, Yosip's words were slightly distorted and the sounds he made were throaty and hoarse, but there was no chance of misunderstanding what he said. "Then someone should take a big iron pot and smash it over your—!"

"Oh, Yosip, Yosip, Yosip," wept Mordecai ben Yahbahbai.

FATHER Nikolai's huge horse was not built for speed, but the mare's thick legs enabled her to walk all day and her broad back could easily support two men. In this case, the two men were the priest and Oleg.

"Why couldn't they wait to be wed until the next time I ride your way? I would have been there in a few months," asked the bearded man.

"They are special people, Father Nikolai. Since anyone can remember, Yuri is the first person who can read in the place where we live. Although only twenty, still a youth, he is the strongest man among us and wise and honorable for his years. He will be our leader soon. Liebeh, his betrothed, is a worthy match for him. But life is short and it is painful when one is young and must wait."

"So they are impatient?"

"No, my Father. They would have waited. They do not know I have come to fetch you. But my fellow woodsmen and I talked it over. Since we are poor and cannot afford to give them an appropriate gift, all we can do is hasten the date of their marriage." Solemnly, Oleg paused, then said, "You, Father Nikolai, are their wedding present."

SHIMKEH pleaded with the old graying nag.

"Please, horse. Faster. Even travelers on foot are passing us by. Faster, please."

But the buggy creaked along at the same wormlike pace. Shimkeh knew that the next time he closed his eyes to sleep, all he would see in his dreams would be a ragged tail and bony rump.

So hard did he concentrate on the horse that for a moment he didn't watch the road ahead, and so it was Froomeh who said, "Water."

"Soon, my orchid, my rose, my tulip. Soon there will be a stream or lagoon and we'll drink."

"Water," she repeated. "I see water."

"You do? Oh, yes! A stream beside the road. Now you and I shall drink."

"The horse," she said.

"The horse?"

"The horse will drink, too."

"Yes! Madonna, mother of the world, I love you. Of course, the horse."

Sensing or smelling the water ahead, the nag quickened its pace somewhat. Soon Shimkeh had steered the creaky vehicle off the road and next to the stream.

As the horse drank, Froomeh and Shimkeh went to their knees, cupped their hands, brought the cool water to their mouths, and drank thirstily.

"Ah," breathed Shimkeh. "Ahhhh—what? What's that? Oh, no!" he exclaimed. He leaped to his feet and stared toward the road.

Thundering toward them, led by a fierce sergeant major, rode a troop of cossacks. They were so near and coming so fast there was no opportunity to run or hide. All Shimkeh had time for was to toss away his cigar.

Petrified, he stood trembling as the soldiers pulled up, dismounted, and led their horses to the water.

"Good day, ladies," the Sergeant Major greeted them.

He glanced at Shimkeh in distaste, but his eyes feasted on beautiful Froomeh.

"G-g-good—d-d-ay," Shimkeh managed to say in a woman's voice.

"And where are you going on such a lovely afternoon?" the Sergeant Major said to Froomeh, doffing his plumed helmet and bowing low to her.

"We are going—we are going—" Trying to remember, Froomeh screwed her features in such an adorable way that the Sergeant Major laughed, delighted.

"This road leads to only two cities, lovely lady. Either you're going to Smolensk or Vitebsk."

"No, that's not it." She sighed.

"The only other spot on this road is the place where nobody stops, and no one goes there," announced the Sergeant Major, sticking out his chest and striking a pose for Froomeh's benefit.

"Yes, that's it. We're going there—to stop nobody—um, the place to stop. Um—the place where nobody stops." She smiled triumphantly at her fabulous memory.

"Aha!" trumpeted the Sergeant Major. "This world is amazingly small, madame. We are also going to the place where nobody stops."

"Oh!" exclaimed Shimkeh.

"I beg your pardon?" the Sergeant Major said.

"Oh, what a warm day," Shimkeh answered.

The Sergeant Major did not like looking at Shimkeh. "This is the most hideous woman I have ever seen; she has a face like a deformed bulldog," he thought. Fascinated with Froomeh's beauty, however, he continued gazing at her.

"Perhaps we shall meet again. In the place where nobody stops," he murmured.

"Perhaps," Froomeh replied.

"But now, alas, we must be on our way. A soldier's life is one of responsibilities, you know." To his men, the Sergeant Major commanded in his most virile voice, "Mount! Platoo-oo-oon, mount!"

Swinging himself up into his saddle, posturing and preening for Froomeh, he unsheathed his sword, pointed it toward the road, and shouted, "Forward at a gallop, *ride!*"

As the cossacks thundered away, the Sergeant Major shouted to Froomeh, "Until we meet again!" and swiftly sprinted to the head of the column. Amid dust clouds rising from the road, the cossacks quickly disappeared.

Shimkeh fell to his knees.

"Whew," he whispered, wiping his forehead with the hem of his dress. But he quickly rose and said, "Come, Froomeh, my one and everlasting love. Come!"

Hardly taking his eyes off the direction in which the cossacks had ridden except to search for and find his cigar, he helped Froomeh into the buggy, grabbed the reins, and, walking ahead of the old horse, pulling it along, he headed back for the road.

Climbing into the vehicle, he said, "Go, horse!" This time, however, he gave it a sharp slap on the rump with his belt.

Froomeh's comely brows wrinkled and she inquired, "Shimkeh?"

"I'm sorry, my distillation of all beauty, but a hornet was on the horse. I tried to kill it before it stung him."

"Shimkeh?" she repeated.

"Yes, my pure and eternal bride?"

"The place where nobody stops is back there. We're going the wrong way."

Shimkeh looked over his shoulder at the cossacks' cloud of dust disappearing on the road behind them and said, "No, my angel, my saint, we're going the right way. We're going back to Vitebsk. I, uh, forgot something. Something, uh, I must, uh, do there."

"Oh. Then we won't see the cossacks in the place where nobody stops?"

"No, my epitome of all that is lovely. We won't see the cossacks in the place where nobody stops."

"AND you should be destroyed by fire!" screamed Yosip the Baker, his eyes bulging, his arms waving, froth and spittle spraying from his mouth. "A fire, a roaring hot fire, hotter than the flames in Hades, and you should burn and burn!"

"Oh, Yosip, Yosip, Yosip," wept Mordecai ben Yahbahbai.

"What?" said Yosip, spinning around and seeing Mordecai. "Oh, it's you."

Magically, the anger left Yosip's face and he smiled somewhat sheepishly. "What are you doing in the woods?"

"What am *I* doing? Yosip the Baker, what are *you* doing? Are you ill? Are you, um, are you feeling bad in your head? Be calm, my dearest comrade. Since I've known you, never have I seen you so angry. Come with me back to the house. Ginzl will give you tea and chicken soup. Liebeh will massage your shoulders and neck. I shall play you a song on the balalaika while you take a nap. And then you will feel better."

"But I feel fine now."

"You feel fine now?"

"Yes."

"Then tell me, why were you screaming and shouting and arguing with the trees, and threatening them?"

"The trees?" Yosip the Baker began to laugh. "I was not threatening the trees. I was threatening the Sergeant Major."

"The Sergeant Major? Aha, the Sergeant Major," Mordecai ben Yahbahbai repeated, thinking that his friend had indeed gone crazy. "The Sergeant Major is here, in the woods?"

"You must be mushy in the head today, Mordecai ben Yahbahbai," chuckled Yosip. "Of course the Sergeant Major is not here in the woods. I'm saying the things that should be said to the Sergeant Major when he comes today."

"No, no, Yosip!" shouted Mordecai ben Yahbahbai, horrified. "If you talk like that to the Sergeant Major, he will beat you again!"

Yosip the Baker laughed. "Of course," he said.

"Of course? He will do more than beat you. He will *kill* you! And how foolish it will be for you to provoke him today."

Shrugging, Yosip the Baker smiled.

Mordecai ben Yahbahbai grasped his friend by the arms and cried, "I am now forty-six years of age! Forty-six!"

"Yes, I know," said Yosip the Baker.

"That means—*I am now too old to serve in the army!* Do you understand? The Sergeant Major no longer wants me! There is no reason for you to lie to him or hide me! There is no reason for him to beat you!"

"Of course," answered Yosip the Baker. Looking at the trees he said, "Sergeant Major, you are an evil man. I'm very angry with you."

"He will arrest you."

Pointing to all the trees, Yosip scolded, "It's wrong for you cossacks to torture and terrify and persecute people who have never harmed anyone."

"But cossacks are soldiers. Soldiers persecute people," said Mordecai ben Yahbahbai, desperately trying to reason with Yosip.

"I was a soldier," answered Yosip calmly. "I didn't persecute anyone. I didn't even hurt anyone. Once, we were fighting the Japanese. It was a foggy day. The fog lifted and in front of me, as near as you are to me right now, stood a Japanese soldier. I raised my rifle and saw his heart in my gunsight. Did I pull the trigger? No. I lowered my weapon. I wasn't afraid. I just couldn't kill. The Japanese soldier bowed to me and turned to run away."

Yosip sighed and went on. "At that moment, a cannon shell burst where he was standing. He was blown up. I hope he didn't think I changed my mind and shot him in the back. But there and then, with the stench of death filling my nostrils and poisoning my soul, I swore that even if other men became animals and killed, I wouldn't do it. I threw my rifle to the ground, went back to the rear, and volunteered to be a cook."

Yosip's voice rose again. He glared at the trees and shouted, "That is why I despise you, Sergeant Major! Do you realize what you've done? Your cruelty has made *me*, a peaceful man, want to be as violent as you are!"

Then as quickly as he had begun to shout, so did he again become soft-spoken and calm. Resolutely folding his arms across his chest, he grinned, turned to Mordecai ben Yahbahbai, and explained.

"If I scream at the trees, if the anger boils out of me until there is none left, I shall not be violent," Yosip said.

"Ah," exclaimed Mordecai ben Yahbahbai, now understanding his friend's ranting and raving. Dancing with happiness and relief, Mordecai ben Yahbahbai sang, "Then you have defeated him! You are still a peaceful man! Your anger has fled! You are still Yosip!"

Yosip the Baker threw back his head and laughed a hearty, life-loving laugh. "Yes. And you are a good friend, Mordecai ben Yahbahbai, even though many times in my dreams I also screamed at you. But have no fear. Today when the Sergeant Major leaves us he will think I worship him."

From his apron pocket Yosip the Baker produced his flask. "A toast to us," he said to Mordecai ben Yahbahbai. "A small drink for a great friendship."

As each took a tiny nip from the flask, Mordecai ben Yahbahbai studied his old friend as if this was the first time they had met.

Then joyfully, arm in arm, chuckling, the two comrades walked home together.

"A toast to us," said Yosip the Baker as each of the friends took a tiny nip from the flask.

15

LED by the Sergeant Major, the platoon of cossacks galloped along our road toward the place where nobody stopped.

When they reached Yosip the Baker's house, the horsemen turned off the wide and deep dirt highway and entered the narrow lane that led to his cottage, just as they had done every previous year on the third day of the seventh month.

Smiling to himself, his waxed mustache twitching in anticipation, the Sergeant Major thought about the small box wrapped in oily brown paper inside his saddlebag.

But as they neared the baker's cottage, he squinted through the July heat, frowned, and held up his hand, ordering his men to halt.

"Glasses," the Sergeant Major ordered. Quickly, the corporal handed him a pair of binoculars.

Focusing the instrument and looking toward Yosip the Baker's house, the Sergeant Major growled, "People are lined up outside the baker's house. Could it be a welcoming committee? Aha, I see a priest."

Lowering the binoculars, he said to the corporal, "Some of them are children. But some of them are adults, men of military age. They may be armed. They may be preparing to resist us and prevent our taking their sons to serve the Czar."

"If a priest is with them, they are certainly armed and ready to fight and die," the corporal said. "Why else would there be a priest?"

"Perhaps," muttered the Sergeant Major.

To his men, the Sergeant Major commanded, "Draw weapons!"

With a harsh rasping of metal, the cossacks drew their swords.

"Approach slowly and with care," ordered the Sergeant Major.

The platoon, weapons ready, cantered toward Yosip the Baker's house.

THERE was indeed a welcoming committee lined up across the front of Yosip the Baker's house. In the center stood the old man himself, leaning on his cane, head high, shoulders back, his abundant silver-white beard almost hiding the bib of his apron.

Next to him stood Mordecai ben Yahbahbai and Ginzl, cradling the infant Rochl, and flanked by Liebeh, Yuri, Dovidl, Fraydl, and Deeneh on one side, and Father Nikolai, Oleg, Ya'akov, Boruch, Simchl, Moishl, Ahvrom Tevyeh, and Timmeh Layeh on the other. Behind them stood every man, woman, and child who lived in the place where nobody stopped.

"They have their swords drawn," whispered Liebeh.

"Do they mean to murder us?" asked Fraydl.

"If they do, I'll kill them first," snarled Dovidl. "I'm going to get my hatchet."

"Stay where you are, my boy, and be peaceful," said Yosip. "Today we have nothing to fear."

"I hope you're right, Yosip the Baker," said Yuri. "I don't like it when men come toward me with weapons at the ready."

"Be calm, my children," Father Nikolai said. "They mean us no harm."

As the cossacks came near and their horses slowed to a walk, Yosip the Baker stepped forward and hailed the Sergeant Major.

"Welcome," he called. "Welcome, your Excellency."

By now the horsemen were close enough to the house for the Sergeant Major to study the group surrounding Yosip the Baker.

"Is it a trick?" asked the corporal.

"No," laughed the Sergeant Major. To Yosip the Baker, he shouted, "Aha, selfish baker. Today you greet me like an old friend. What kind of sly peasant game are you playing? Beware. You know I am quick to anger."

"Greetings from the people of this place, your Excellency. All men here of military age are woodchoppers already in the service of the Czar. We have gathered to celebrate a wedding—and to welcome you and your men."

"Humph," snorted the Sergeant Major. To his men he ordered, "Sheathe your weapons!"

Yosip the Baker bowed and continued. "I wish to introduce to you our new schoolmaster. His name is Mordecai ben Yahbahbai, and he formerly taught in a boys' school in Vitebsk. We are very fortunate to have him, Excellency."

"I do not approve of schoolmasters," growled the Sergeant Major. "Teachers? Bah! They think the world is made of words on pieces of paper. The world is made of steel and gunpowder and blood."

Through narrowed eyes, he made a withering examination of Mordecai ben Yahbahbai.

"Step forward, ben Yahbamor," commanded the Sergeant Major.

Bowing as he stepped forward, Mordecai ben Yahbahbai said, softly, "My name, exalted eminence, is Mordecai ben—"

"Never mind what your name is," roared the Sergeant Major. "The names of all your kind sound alike to me." From his lordly height astride his horse, he stared down at Mordecai ben Yahbahbai and coldly demanded, "Hand over your papers."

"Yes, most noble master." From his inside coat pocket, Mordecai ben Yahbahbai took a certificate. Bowing, he handed it to the Sergeant Major.

Without looking at it, the Sergeant Major haughtily gave the parchment to the corporal, who unfolded the document and examined it.

"Well?" snapped the Sergeant Major. "Do we clamp this pitiful specimen in irons and take him with us?"

"According to his birth certificate, issued by the Czar's Ministry of Births and Deaths in the city of Vitebsk, this man was born in the year of Our Lord eighteen hundred and sixty, forty-six years ago," answered the corporal. "He is too old for the army, sir."

"Too bad," grumbled the Sergeant Major. "And you,

boy," he barked, pointing at Dovidl. "How old are you, son of a dog?"

"He is nine years of age, and still a child," Ginzl said, in a voice as sharp as the Sergeant Major's sword. "And he is not the son of a dog. I am his mother."

Smirking, the Sergeant Major stood up in his stirrups and bowed, mocking Ginzl, and sneered, "My deepest apologies, good lady." To Dovidl he growled, "Nine, eh? Very well. We can wait. In seven years, little one, when you are sixteen, you will be ours, and we will come and get you. What do you say to that, mother's boy?"

"I would be a good soldier. I'm not afraid," answered Dovidl, boldly.

"Ho, ho! I like your backbone. Because you stand up like a man, I shall not cut you up in little pieces and feed you to the blackbirds."

"Nor will you come and get him in seven years," Ginzl said, her words hurtling toward the Sergeant Major like bullets.

Suddenly everyone became quiet. It was very dangerous to defy an officer of the Czar.

Glaring at her, the Sergeant Major snarled, "And why will he not be mine when he is sixteen, woman?"

Her shoulders back, standing as tall as one of his soldiers, Ginzl bravely replied, "Because my boy is the eldest son in this family."

The Sergeant Major's frown turned into a disdainful leer. Once more he bowed to her and barked, "Then he is exempt, madam. But if you have other sons, be certain we shall take them when they are of age."

Again turning his attention to Yosip the Baker, the Sergeant Major paused, stared at the white-haired man, and finally said, "As for you, you greedy, selfish old miser, I am going to show you how the glorious army of the Czar forgives those who refuse to feed its soldiers. Instead of a thrashing, you old billy goat, I have something different for you today. A gift. You deny my men food, and yet I bring you a gift."

Dismounting, the Sergeant Major opened his saddlebag and took from it the small box wrapped in oily brown paper.

"I did not know there was a wedding today, or I would have brought a gift for the bride, too. But this is for you. Here, take it."

"I thank your Excellency," said Yosip the Baker, examining the package.

"Well? Well? Unwrap it," ordered the Sergeant Major.

"Yes, Excellency," said Yosip the Baker. Slowly, carefully, he untied the string. When all the wrapping was loosened, he reached within the folds of paper, removed what was inside, and held it out for all to see.

In his open palm, gleaming in the bright sunlight, was a set of false teeth.

Everyone, including the cossacks, gasped in admiration. Never had there been teeth as sparkling white as these. They were made of shiny, highly polished porcelain. Never had gums been so magnificently red. They were made of crimson-colored rubber.

For a few seconds, they all gazed at the dentures resting in Yosip's hand. The front teeth were slightly parted, as if waiting either to say something or chew something. They seemed to be smiling.

Proudly, the Sergeant Major said, "A captain in my

regiment just died. When I saw the teeth he left behind, I thought of you, Baker, and purchased them from his widow."

Still dumbfounded, still staring at the teeth in his hand, Yosip replied, "I thank you, Excellency."

"Well? Well? Put them in your mouth. See how they fit. Then let me hear you say something. Let me see you eat something," the Sergeant Major commanded.

As everyone watched, fascinated, Yosip the Baker stuffed the dentures, first the lower, then the upper, into his mouth. Remarkably, they fit reasonably well.

"Written on the wrapping paper is the name of a barber in Vitebsk who is also a maker of teeth," the Sergeant Major said. "If these dentures do not fit well, I have commanded him to adjust them free of charge."

Bowing, Yosip the Baker again said, "I thank you, Excellency." When he straightened up and grinned, the sun glinted off his teeth, making the inside of his mouth whiter than his beard.

"They make you look very handsome," boasted the Sergeant Major. "You should be pleased, old man. When you refused to feed my men, it was my duty as a soldier to knock your teeth out. Now I give you new ones. But I hope you have learned your lesson, Baker."

For a frigid moment, he stared at Yosip the Baker. Finally, in a deadly voice, he said, "And now, Baker, do you have something to say to me besides thank you?"

"Yes, your Excellency," replied Yosip the Baker, his words whistling a bit through his new teeth. "I have a great deal to say to you."

"Oh, no!" thought Mordecai ben Yahbahbai. "He's going to tell the Sergeant Major what he thinks of him!"

But Mordecai ben Yahbahbai was incorrect.

Yosip the Baker proudly put his hands below his round belly, lifted until his chest stuck out, and said, "To express my gratitude, please allow me the pleasure of inviting you and your men to share the wedding feast we have prepared."

The cossacks shouted their approval, dismounted, and tethered their mounts near the water trough.

Very pleased with himself, the Sergeant Major turned to the corporal and said, "I hope you have learned this lesson well. First I teach the baker to fear my whip. Then I pay two kopeks for a set of discarded false teeth, give them to the addlebrained old donkey as a gift, and in his gratitude, he is now our slave. Peasants may be bought cheaply. And, as you see, he loves me."

"Yes, sir!" replied the corporal, clicking his heels and saluting. "It is a good lesson."

"A man who has been a soldier for twenty-five years, as I have, becomes very wise," said the Sergeant Major. "And now come inside and taste the best babka and bread ever created by man."

AS far back as anyone could recall, never had there been so festive and memorable an event in the place where nobody stopped as that third day of the seventh month in the year 1906.

The celebration of Yuri and Liebeh's marriage lasted into the night. Finally, knowing they must rise before dawn and work the next day in the heat of summer, the people of the place where nobody stopped went to their

houses and, savoring the beauty of the wedding day, slept happily.

Yuri and Liebeh shyly and lovingly said good-night and retired to the small bedroom Yosip had built for her, where they would spend their first night together as man and wife. All of Liebeh's brothers and sisters, except for Dovidl, had long since been put to bed in their own tiny rooms.

Now the house was quiet. Yosip the Baker, Ginzl, and Mordecai ben Yahbahbai, our three old friends, sat at the big table and smiled at each other in the afterglow of the day's joy.

Dovidl sat on his mother's lap, trying to stay awake. He'd never been up this late. Suddenly, however, his sleepy eyes opened wide and he stood up.

Walking toward Liebeh's door, he said, "I forgot to tell Liebeh and Yuri good-night."

"Not so fast, boychik," his father said, laughing. "I advise you to wait until morning to tell them good-night."

"Yes, Dovidl," smiled Ginzl. "This is not a good time to disturb them. Kiss me and go to bed."

GINZL and Mordecai ben Yahbahbai bade Yosip the Baker good-night and went into their room.

On the night of the third day of the seventh month in the year 1906, Yosip the Baker's house was once again quiet.

Although his heart overflowed with happiness, the aged baker's body also was overwhelmed—with weariness. The excitement of this long, hot summer day had drained him to the point of exhaustion.

Nevertheless, there was something he had to do.

Moving slowly and with great effort, he fetched kindling from the woodpile just outside the door.

This was a strange thing to do on a steaming July night. Today had been the Sabbath, so he hadn't prepared the dough for tomorrow's baking. Each Monday morning, however, he always rose earlier and, with Ginzl's help, mixed, measured, kneaded, and shaped the loaves. Only then did he need a fire in the great stone oven.

But Yosip doggedly brought wood, two or three pieces at a time, and expertly placed them in the chamber below the oven. When he was satisfied, he threw in some shavings, struck a match, lit the chips, and then sat down, fatigued, and waited for the fire to snap and blaze. He didn't have to wait long. The summer wood was dry, and within minutes the furnace roared.

Our old friend rose from his chair, walked to the oven, opened the door to the fire chamber, and for a moment stood and watched the dancing orange flames.

Finally, he took out his false teeth, took one last look at them, then tossed them into the inferno.

It took only a few seconds for the red rubber to warp, distort, and finally burst into yellow flames and melt. The porcelain teeth blackened as they scattered and fell to the bottom of the furnace and began to crack and explode, dancing in the heat like popping kernels of corn.

Yosip the Baker rubbed his hands together, as if he were wiping something filthy off them. Then he closed the iron door of the great stone oven, blew out the light from the kerosene lamp, lay his weary body on his cot, smiled back at the moon peeping in through the window, fell immediately into a deep slumber, and slept the sleep of a good and loving man in the place where nobody stopped.

THE END

Afterthoughts

JUST because someone prints "The End" at the bottom of my story, is it really the end?

When you finish reading the final page or listen to the last words, should everything freeze in time and stay that way forever?

Yes and no.

Yes, because I want you to remember Yosip the Baker as we left him.

Yes, I want you to close your eyes and see the place where nobody stopped as it was in our story.

But—and as Mordecai ben Yahbahbai would say, this is a very big but—can our story ever truly end?

Dirt roads become paved. Automobiles and trains replace horses and carriages. Czars are killed, cossacks defeated, governments overthrown.

Nine-year-old boys grow into men. Young newlyweds move from villages to cities. Babies are born. People we love die. Families travel across oceans and settle in new worlds. Scoundrels surprise us and make us laugh. Poets touch us and make us cry. Life is a continuing adventure.

And the end is not always the end.